NENE CAPRI
PRESENTS

LATE NIGHT LICK VOLUME 4 PRESENTS HIDDEN EXSTASY

A Novel By
Chastity Adams

HIDDEN EXSTASY

CHASTITY ADAMS

Chapter One

Shonda pulled up in front of the dark brown log cabin. She turned down *Kelly Rowland's Motivation*. Then dead her engine and parked in the designated spot he'd reserved just for her. Shonda took a minute to enjoy the view of the beautiful, sunsetting that illuminated in the flowing water of the lake, directly across from the cabin. The sounds of, birds chirping and crickets stirring in the distance calmed her spirit.

Shonda reached over into the passenger seat and grabbed her purse. She freshened her lip gloss and scented her skin. She took one last look in her rearview mirror and fingered through her hair before popping the locks. She got out of the car, opened the back door, and retrieved her duffle bag and briefcase. A sudden sense of guilt rushed over her, as she stepped onto the porch, loudly knocked on the door and patiently waited.

"Well, damn, aren't you sight for sore eyes?" He remarked after opening the door, admiring how her dark blue leggings looked as though they were glued to her smooth, caramel skin, showing off her curves and thighs perfectly.

"I could say the same about you," Shonda replied entering the cabin, unable to take her eyes off him.

He stood there covered in a large red towel, with tiny drops of water running down his chiseled torso. The guilt Shonda previously felt instantly disappeared. Her body tingled and her pussy throbbed, as her eyes fixated on his dark cocoa skin.

"I had to jump in the shower, thought I'd be dressed before you got here." He responded rubbing his hand over his goatee.

"That's fine, Larenzo," Shonda answered, not bothered at all.

"Okay, well, guess I should invite you in huh?" Larenzo joked.

Shonda tilted her head, and a smirk curved her lips, "Yeah, that would be nice."

"Let me get that for you." Larenzo reached down, taking her duffle bag out of her hand. Then he noticed her briefcase in her other hand. "I don't know why you brought that, darling? Trust me you won't be needing it."

"Well, if my excuse for being out of town was going to be work-related. I had to bring my work with me, Larenzo duh," She commented smartly.

"Whatever get your ass in here." He sat her bag down by the door in the living room.

Shonda shut the door and locked it, then followed him into the living room.

"I am all yours this weekend, baby girl." Larenzo faced her and dropped his towel, releasing his already hard thickness.

Shonda gawked at his nakedness. Before she could speak, he closed the space between them, grabbed her face, briefly gazed into her hazel eyes and kissed her intensely. As their tongues wrestled, he rubbed his hands over her breasts, through her long-sleeved, black sheer crop top, then let them travel down, under her skirt.

"I see somebody been waiting for me." Larenzo teased slipping a finger inside her wetness.

"I guess you been waiting for me, too?" Shonda replied grabbing his manhood and squeezing it until it throbbed in the palm of her hand.

"Take your clothes off and meet me in the bedroom." He whispered in her ear.

Larenzo let Shonda go and turned to exit the living room. Shonda kicked off her shoes and eased out of her leggings and top. She moved quickly in Larenzo's direction stepping out of her thong along the way.

Shonda blushed and giggled when she entered the bedroom and saw all that he had taken the time to do just for her. There were scented candles set strategically around the room with small flames dancing on top of each one. The black and red silk curtains covering the windows blew lightly next to the bed. Her feet sank into the matching plush red carpet with every step tickling her bare-feet and toes.

Her eyes grew wide when she saw Larenzo standing in the middle of the room dangling a pair of red cloth covered cuffs in one hand and a black blindfold in the other hand.

"Welcome to your weekend." She teased as she pulled at the cuffs from both sides.

Shonda's face lit up when she saw the black, Queen-sized bed and the black sheer curtains on the canopy top joined together by four mahogany bed posts with gold balls at the tip. On top of the thick mattress lay a huge plush red comforter which made her want to wrap herself in it. Her heart melted as she heard J. Holiday's 'It's Yours' crooning throughout the room, setting the mood just right.

The flames crackled, inside the red brick fireplace as the night began to get just as heated.

"You remembered?" Shonda's lightly nodded her head along with the music.

"Of course, I told you unlike that lame you got at home, I listen to my woman," he remarked boastfully.

Shonda took a deep breath, "Larenzo if this is going to work I'm going to need you to refrain from talking about my man."

Larenzo raised his hands in surrender, he wasn't trying to ruin the moment, he'd spent weeks planning for. "Alright Baby Girl, you got that," he assured.

"So, now what?" Shonda asked getting back to the cuffs and blindfold.

"Whatever you want baby…whatever you want!" Larenzo said taking her hand, leading her over to the bed.

As they walked to the bed they enjoyed the light summer breeze from the slightly cracked double glass doors. Shonda was clueless of what the night would bring, she had many desires that she longed to act out. However, had never been in a position to execute any of them until now. Here she was with a man who was pleasurably different from any man she'd ever known, including the man she loved.

Shonda closed the space between them, threw her hands around his neck, and feverishly tongued him.

"Damn, you so fuckin' thick," Larenzo said caressing her thighs, licking his lips.

Everything about her turned him on, she was the perfect level of thickness for his taste. He grabbed her apple shaped ass and pulled her close to him. He could feel the nipples getting hard as her plump 38C cup breasts pressed against him.

"Don't worry, I'ma take good care of you. Do you trust me?" Larenzo said. Shonda nodded nervously. "Good now turn around," he demanded.

Shonda did as he asked and turned her back to him. She could feel the warmth of his six-foot-two frame towering over her, and his breath on the nape of her neck, as he carefully slid the blindfold over her eyes. After making sure the blindfold was tight and secure, he guided her over to the bed, onto the soft, red, silk sheets. As Shonda laid down she couldn't see anything except darkness, but she could feel everything he was doing to her.

Shonda's body tensed up as she felt the furry steel tightening as he cuffed her wrists to the bedposts. She felt her legs being spread apart as his cold hands caressed her luscious thighs.

"Relax baby, I got you," he whispered. Larenzo's hands, caressed up and down her skin, mesmerized by her curves. "Damn, you thick as hell," He commented once again.

Shonda's breathing escalated, as she felt him ease between her legs. Larenzo's hands roamed over her full breasts, then he started sucking one as he squeezed the other. He teased her stiff nipples with the tip of his tongue then rolled them gently between his teeth.

Shonda's body shivered as his hands traveled along her body, on down to her sweet spot. He slipped two fingers inside her wetness and tickled until her hips began to ride to his touch.

"Mmmh…" Shonda moaned as his fingers plunged harder and deeper, causing her to become wetter and hotter.

"You like that?" Larenzo asked Shonda nodded. "Unh-unh…I wanna hear you say it loud and clear." He demanded and started fingering her even faster.

Larenzo twirled his two fingers around in circles while flicking his thumb over her pulsating clit.

"Yyyess…baby, I…I…like it!" Shonda moaned louder.

Larenzo knew she was about to cum by the way her legs began to tremble, so he stopped, and yanked his fingers out.

"W…why'd you…sss…stop?" Shonda panted.

"It's not time yet," Larenzo replied. "Don't worry sweetheart. You will not be disappointed once I'm finished.

Shonda didn't say another word, she just laid there agreeing to let Larenzo have his way with her. She'd asked for this moment, and he was ready to deliver, so all she could do was embrace it, with no regrets.

"You scared?" Larenzo asked sensing hesitation in her.

Shonda nervously laughed, "Never scared, just a little nervous."

"Don't be, I got you…now relax."

"Okay…okay!" Shonda answered.

Larenzo reached over onto the night-stand where he'd placed a bottle of honey and a silver ice bucket just before she arrived. He opened the bottle, held it up, and drizzled it over her breasts, stomach, then all over her neatly shaved box. Shonda's body was filled with goosebumps as she felt the cool liquid being poured over her throbbing clit.

Once the honey was saturated to his liking, Larenzo grabbed an ice cube out of the bucket. Shonda's skin was hot to the touch, Larenzo knew the ice would be a great addition to his foreplay.

Larenzo rolled the cube of ice back and forth over her nipples attending to one after the other. Shonda's body trembled, and her heart drummed against her chest with every chilling drip onto her hot skin.

"Aahhh…Laren…Larenzo, it's…it's cold." Shonda moaned barely able to speak. Her breathing increased, causing her stomach to heave up and down.

Larenzo didn't respond, his hands eased down, moving the ice from her breasts, down to her belly button, blending it with the sweet honey. He repeated the motion until he was back up to her breasts.

"Oohhh…God…" Shonda moaned louder, her entire body shook, chills shot up and down her spine, and heat surged through her, despite Larenzo's ice cold taunting.

Larenzo put the ice in his mouth, then began making his way down to her sweet spot. He held the ice on his tongue as he covered her entire clit with his mouth and gently sucked. Shonda raised up off the bed, then back down, realizing she was incapable of going anywhere.

"D…damn…baby…" she squealed.

Larenzo's taste buds awakened, as the ice, honey, and Shonda's juices meshed in his mouth. Once the ice had melted. He licked and kissed her body, from her belly button to her breasts, from her breasts back down to her stomach, careful not to leave any passion marks, knowing she had a man to go home to. Once he'd devoured all the honey, he made his way back down, to finish what he'd started.

"Oooh…sss…shit…" Shonda moaned, swaying her hips to the motion of his tongue action and finger thrusting. "Eat that pussy…" she shrieked, wanting so badly to grab the back of his head and hold him in place.

Larenzo nibbled on her clit harder, plunging his fingers deeper. As he went from nibbling to intense sucking, Shonda's body started to convulse, she closed her thighs around his neck. Larenzo used the strength of his other arm and pried her legs back open. As he felt her about to release, he stopped.

"W…what you doing?" Shonda panted.

Larenzo didn't respond, in a swift motion he raised her legs up on his shoulders and entered her slippery wetness. He slow stroked her until his iron hard, curved dick was half-way inside her. As her pussy stretched to accommodate his length, he started fucking her hard and fast, hitting her walls intensely.

"Aaah…Larenz…Larenzo, work that dick baby. Oooh…God…fuck me!" Shonda screamed, working her hips, causing him to speed his strokes.

"Hell, yeah give me that pussy! This dick feels good, huh?" Larenzo moaned. Shonda nodded, as he felt an orgasm rising, he stopped, pulled his dick out, and got off the bed. Just as Shonda was about to say something, he put his finger over her lips. "I got this," He said, moving to the top of the bed, uncuffing her wrists, then to the bottom uncuffing her ankles.

"Follow me," Larenzo told her.

"Follow you where?" Shonda asked, sitting all the way up, snatching off the blindfold.

Her eyes followed him, as he exited the double doors, walked over to the square Jacuzzi hot tub, and slowly sunk into the water.

"Come on woman, it's nice out here!" Larenzo said louder, stretching his arms on the side of the hot tub.

Shonda wasn't sure if this was a good idea. The breeze had gotten cooler since she first arrived, and her legs still shook from the euphoria she'd just experienced.

"Well, I did say I wanted to switch things up." She reminded herself. "Alright, I'm coming," she called back.

As she stood up, slowly getting off the bed, making her way out onto the patio, her legs were weak with pleasure. Once she managed to get out onto the patio, Larenzo, stood up, took her hand, and escorted inside the hot tub.

Larenzo, scooped her in his arms, sitting her on the edge of the tub. Shonda looked up into the sky, at the bright stars and shining moon, as he started sucking on her neck. As she suspected the temperature had dropped, but the heat from the bubbling water, masked the cold wind.

"It's so...so nice out here," Shonda stuttered.

"Uh...huh," Larenzo mumbled, now sucking her breasts, shoving three fingers inside her wetness.

"Aahhh..." Shonda screamed, her walls tensed up and tightened around his fingers.

"Relax," Larenzo instructed.

He took his fingers out, replacing them with his dick. He teased her center, slipping his dick in, then back out, repeatedly.

"Shit...Larenzo, you keep this up...damn boy!" She moaned slightly lifting her waist, to meet his strokes.

"Aahhh...this pussy feels so good," Larenzo, groaned lifting her legs out of the water, onto his shoulders. As his strokes intensified, he gripped her shoulders while looking into her eyes. "Spread that pussy for me?" he requested.

Shonda reached under her, spreading her ass cheeks wide. Larenzo, plunged fast and deep, attacking her walls with precision.

"Ooohh…shit give it to me baby!" Shonda begged.

"You want it all, huh?" Larenzo asked.

"Yes daddy, I…I want…want it all." Shonda confirmed.

Larenzo, stared deep into her eyes, pushing all his inches inside wetness per her request.

"Shit, I'm cumming in this pus…" Before he could finish he exploded. "Turn around," he instructed.

Shonda didn't say anything as she quickly complied, stepping down into the water, turning her back to him and settling into his embrace.

"You trust me, right?" Larenzo asked again. Shonda nodded. "Good girl," He replied, kissing the small of her back.

He pushed her forward until her back was arched perfectly. Larenzo tightly gripped the back of her neck. "Open your legs wide," he instructed.

Shonda opened her legs wide as he entered her.

Larenzo slammed all his inches deep inside of her. He kept one leg firmly on the bottom of the hot tub and put one leg up on the side of the hot tub. As he went to work inside her pussy, he released his grip on her neck, and held her ass, spreading it open. He stuck two fingers in his mouth, then slipped them inside her asshole.

"Aaah…uuunnh…" Shonda squealed, trying to move.

Using his free hand, Larenzo pulled her back into him, fucking her harder, while twirling his fingers faster inside her asshole. "Where you going…huh?" he groaned. "Stop trying to run, take this shit! You wanted it right?" Larenzo said refusing to let up.

Shonda's body and mind felt like it was spinning out of control, she'd never felt pleasure of this magnitude.

"Aahhh…shit…you…you driving me crazy," She cried, throwing her pussy back into him. "That feels so fucking good!" she screamed.

"Whose pussy is this?" Larenzo asked fucking her harder.

"Yours baby…oooh…baby, it's yours," She squealed louder, as her body quivered.

Larenzo pulled his fingers out of her ass and clutched her shoulders tight with both hands, pushing so hard inside her, his nuts slammed into her ass. He held her tighter as his body began to shake along with hers and they exploded together.

Shonda collapsed on the side of the hot tub, struggling to catch her breath, Larenzo collapsed on her back, letting his dick fall out of her.

"Damn your pussy good! Um…um your man don't know how lucky he is!" Larenzo commented.

"What I tell you about that shit?" Shonda panted, shooting her eyes back at him. "Don't ruin a good moment."

"You right…sorry," Larenzo agreed.

Larenzo released her shoulders and she tried to relax as she was still wrapped in the adrenaline rush from their powerful orgasms. As Larenzo stepped out of the hot tub, he took her hand, helped her out, then scooped her into his arms. He carried her back into the room, laying her down on the bed, so she could regroup while he went to take a shower.

"You're free to join me if you want!" Larenzo called from the bathroom.

"Be there in a minute," Shonda agreed, letting her mind replay the night.

She knew she was wrong and that everything she was doing could possibly blow up in her face. However, at the moment she was in no position to care or complain.

Larenzo's dick filled her insides just right with every stroke. The orgasms he gave her were the most intense she'd ever felt, and unlike other men. He listened to her body and executed all her desires, no matter how big or small, no questions asked.

Chapter Two

"Shit…baby your pussy…pussy so good!" He moaned, pumping hard and fast.

"You feel good, too!" Shonda moaned softly, closing her eyes, wrapping her legs tighter around his waist. "Roman baby…"

Shonda had been back home less than twenty-four hours when Roman woke her up for a late-night quickie. She couldn't tell him, she was too sore from her weekend rendezvous to comply, otherwise, he'd know something was wrong.

"Y…yeah, baby?" Roman moaned into her ear. "Speak up when you talking to Daddy!" he suggested.

Shonda held onto Roman's milk cocoa-colored face, stared into his hazel eyes, and passionately kissed him. "Do it harder baby," She begged a little louder.

Roman kept stroking missionary style, kissing the side of Shonda's neck, ignoring her request as his orgasm began to rise, and her legs started to tremble.

"Aaah…I'm…I'm cumming!" Roman moaned letting loose.

Shonda appreciated the fact that Roman was adamant about making sure she got her orgasm, but as of late she needed more, and the time was nearing for Roman to step up and deliver. Roman laid in Shonda's arm, as she rubbed the back of his head gently.

"Roman, we need to talk," she said.

Roman continued ignoring her and closed his eyes, drifting off to sleep. He knew she wanted more sexually, he just didn't think she'd be able to handle him dicking her down the way he did prior females. So, his best bet, for now, was to play it safe."

"Roman…I know you hear me?" Shonda looked down at him.

"Can we please talk later? I'm tired and I have a busy day tomorrow," Roman stated.

Shonda sighed heavily, "Sure, whatever."

****

Shonda arrived at her office, Lawrence and Warren Real Estates, and confided in her best friend and business partner Nina, first thing the next morning. She'd just explained to her how much she needed a change in her and Roman's sexual relationship.

"I'm having a hard time seeing the problem," Nina responded after hearing Shonda out.

"Don't get me wrong, Nina, I love Roman. His dick fills me up just right and he always makes sure I'm taken care of, but…"

"But, what sounds like good times to me, Shonda!" Nina assumed cutting her off.

"I just wish we had more spark you know. I want him to give me that neck gripping, ass smacking, intense fucking. You know handcuff to me to the bed, pull my hair, stick his finger in my ass type shit. Why does our sex lives have to be so complex?" Shonda complained.

"Girl, when did you become Anastasia Steele? I've never heard you talk like this before, what has…or should I say who has gotten into you lately?" Nina stated curiously.

"Nothing…no one," Shonda lied. "I'm just bored with things the way they are in the bedroom. I'm tired of playing the shy, good girl all the damn time." Shonda pushed the brim of her reading glasses up on her nose and glared at Nina. "I'm ready to be wild and dangerous for a change," she admitted.

"Have you told him this?" Nina questioned.

"I tried, but he ignored me and fell asleep." Shonda sighed and started loudly tapping her freshly manicured nails on the mahogany wooden desk.

"You think maybe he wants what you want but is afraid you won't go for it or you're not ready. Why don't you test him and see where his head is at?" Nina suggested.

Shonda thought about that for a moment, "You know what Nina that's a good idea. Then maybe I can dictate the boundaries of pleasure."

"Yeah, but if he doesn't go for it and is unwilling to see things your way. What are you going to do?" Nina questioned.

"Nina, all I can do is tolerate it and get mines the best way I can," Shonda confessed, then quickly looked down at her desk so Nina wouldn't be able to read anything else brewing in her eyes.

"Well, I have to get back to work," Nina said.

"Thanks, Nina, I'll let you know what I plan to do later," Shonda said as Nina got up, headed for the door.

Nina nodded, then exited her office, shutting the door behind her. As Shonda started going over the schedule for the week her mind roamed. She had to figure out a way to let Roman know she was ready for more. She knew he took baby steps with her sexually because he didn't want to lose the quiet, shy, laid back chick he fell in love with.

Unfortunately, unbeknownst to his knowledge that girl had been gone for months. Despite this truth, however,

Shonda knew in order to keep Roman happy and not draw suspicion she'd have to continue playing her role for now. In the meantime, she'd just get a taste of pain with much-added pleasure from Larenzo.

After work as Shonda was on her way home, she received a text from Roman.

//: *It's been a long day, daddy needs his baby girl to come over and make him feel better. ~Roman~*

She smiled, just as she was about to respond, another text message came through.

//: *Can't stop thinking about you, baby I miss you. Wish you could come and give me some of them sweet walls. I'm in town for the next couple of days on business. If you down, let me know and I'll text you my hotel info. ~Larenzo~*

All Shonda could do was blush. She had two handsome chocolate, sexy, hardworking men going crazy over her. In her mind, she had the best of both worlds. When she was with one she was laid back and reserved and allowed him to take charge. When she's with the other one he gave her the freedom to be free and open to all kinds of sexual adventures.

Shonda went home, showered, changed, and headed over to Roman's house.

"Whoa, what's going on in here?" Shonda asked aloud after letting herself into the house with her extra key.

The scent of lit candles and the aroma of delicious food hit her nose with force.

Roman came out of the kitchen and approached her with a hug and kiss. "I'm glad you came," He said pulling her into his arms, caressing the small of her back.

"Did I miss some kind of special event or something?" Shonda asked curiously.

"Nope," Roman replied. "I told you I was going to cook for you one day. Well, today is that day baby," Roman stated.

Shonda lightly chuckled. "After six months Roman really?" She questioned jokingly.

"Whatever, woman, just come on," Roman said taking her by the hand.

"Let me wash my hands first," Shonda said pulling away from him.

Roman let go of her hand and she dipped into the half bathroom by the living room and washed her hands. Then he led her into his dining room and pulled out her chair. After she sat down at the round espresso colored dining table, he pushed the chair back in and took the seat across from her. In the middle of the table sat a white roast pan containing two large juicy medium rare steaks, another pan that contained four loaded baked potatoes, and a huge crystal-clear bowl that contained a tossed vegetable salad. Next to the bowl on each side was a bottle of olive oil and balsamic vinaigrette dressing.

"I love you...I'm a lucky man," Roman commented.

"So, I've heard," Shonda replied, remembering Larenzo's words.

"Well, let's eat so daddy can get to his dessert!" Roman replied licking his lips. "Ladies first," He said pointing to the food.

Shonda began filling her plate with the salad and baked potato first. She didn't want all of Roman's efforts to go in vain, so she cut half of one of the steaks and put it on a separate plate.

"This looks and smells amazing, Roman. Now how it's going to taste is a different story," Shonda joked.

"Oh, I see you got jokes." Roman nodded. "We'll see who's laughing in a little bit." He reached his hand over and slid it up her thigh.

Shonda's body shivered as Roman's cool hands eased up her sundress. Roman slid his fingers up and down the thin fabric of her panties until warmth and wetness oozed from her center.

"You...you keep this up, we're not going to make it through dinner." Shonda managed to say as his middle finger entered her opening through the side of her panties.

"I'm counting on it," Roman said staring into her eyes.

He pushed his finger in and out, then rotated until her pussy juices dripped down on his hand. He pulled his hand away, got up from the table, and went into the hall bathroom to wash his hands.

Shonda sat there, her legs shaking, and her pussy on fire, begging for more. "Why...why'd you stop?" She asked Roman when he returned to the table.

"Just a tease before the main course baby," Roman stated, sitting down, cutting into his steak. He shot her a sneaky grin.

"Oh, okay," Shonda replied, she lifted her heel underneath the table and kicked his leg.

"Owe...what...what the fuck?" Roman yelped.

"That's for teasing Miss Kitty like that!" Shonda stated returning his sneaky grin.

"You gon' pay for that," Roman warned, with a head nod.

"Oh, I'm counting on it." Shonda giggled.

****

HIDDEN EXSTASY

After dinner, Shonda and Roman headed upstairs, as soon as he closed the door behind them. Shonda undid his tie and snatched it off, then she unbuttoned his dark blue collared shirt and removed it, exposing his pulsating muscles. Roman's six-foot-two frame towered over her as he stood there smiling from ear to ear.

"I have a surprise for you," Roman told Shonda heading for his closet.

When Roman came back out of the closet, he placed two boxes on the edge of the bed and stood there watching as she tore into each one anxiously.

"Ooh, Roman…" Shonda shrieked.

She pulled her gift out of the first box and spread it out on the bed. It was a beautiful, sexy lingerie outfit, in her favorite color; royal blue.

"I love it," Shonda replied smiling.

"I'm going to take a shower, you don't have to open the second one if you don't want too," Roman stated heading for the bathroom.

"No, I want to see what it is," Shonda affirmed.

When Roman returned from the bathroom, Shonda was standing at the edge of the bed, dressed in the lingerie outfit, holding the 'Beat Me Please' tickling whip he'd bought, looking like she was ready to do damage. Roman eyed her seductively, slowly licking his lips, he was immediately turned on.

"What you think you're doing with that?" He questioned pointing at the whip.

"I assume you bought it to heat things up a bit," Shonda answered, shaking the whip, causing it to snap.

"You ain't ready for that baby girl," Roman complained.

He walked over to her, grabbed her hand, and removed the whip, dropping it to the floor. Then he grabbed her breasts squeezing them tight.

"Why'd you buy it then, Roman?" Shonda was becoming irritated.

"A lack of judgment I guess. I like you just the way you are baby," Roman confessed.

He fell to his knees and started slowly kissing her stomach, then he kissed each one of her thighs. He came back up, slid the dark blue laced thong down, started sucking on clit, and slipped his middle finger in her wetness. Roman lifted one leg up on his shoulder and started sucking and fingering her faster.

"Uuunhhh…Roman!" Shonda moaned.

Roman's tongue was lethal, and she relished in the pleasure every chance she got. Shonda held the back of his head and started gyrating up and down to the motion of his fingers.

"Don't stop, baby!" She moaned, then threw her head back, gasping with pleasure.

Her body started shivering as an orgasm began to rise. Roman sucked her clit and fingered her faster.

"Aaahh…do it harder, baby," Shonda begged and Roman complied. "Sss…shit!" She yelled as her orgasm squirted all over Roman's tongue and face.

"Now it's your turn," Roman demanded as he got up off the floor. "Make Daddy come." He grabbed her head pushing her down onto the floor.

Shonda dropped to her knees, grabbed his shaft, and started stroking it to full capacity.

"Mmm…that's what I'm talking about," Roman said holding her head as she licked around the tip, then put half of his inches in her mouth. As she began bobbing her head up and down in a rhythmic motion Roman held her head tighter.

"Aahhh…shit suck that dick, baby," He moaned, throwing his head back, pushing his dick in and out of her wet mouth.

His leg began to shake as his climax rose. He held her head even tighter and pushed all his inches in her mouth until he unloaded deep in the back of her throat.

"Sss…shit, baby…damn…" Roman breathed, pulling his dick out of her mouth, giving her a satisfied look.

"You liked that?" Shonda asked getting off the floor.

"Loved it," Roman replied kissing her.

"Good. Now time for round two!" She picked the whip back up off the floor.

"Didn't I tell you to put that down?" Roman questioned sternly.

"Why can't we at least try it, Roman?" Shonda was getting irritated.

"I already told you why," he fussed. "Shonda discussion's over, if you want Christian Grey, I suggest you go find his ass. Now, where were we?" Roman, closed the space between them, pulled her into his arms, and eased her over to the bed, laying her down.

Shonda didn't feel like arguing, she just wanted to get the night over with. She opened her legs and positioned the tip of Roman's dick at her slit. He entered her slowly as his dick grew hard again. Shonda laid there looking into the ceiling as he pumped in and out enjoying every minute. She moved her hips as quickly as she could in an effort to make him cum faster.

"Aaahhh…you feel so good. I love you, baby!" Roman moaned releasing inside of her.

Shonda didn't say anything she just kissed him. When he got off her, it didn't take long for him to fall asleep. This gave Shonda the perfect time to make a much-needed move. She gathered her things, dressed, and gave Roman one last kiss.

"I love you, Roman, no matter what." She whispered in his ears, then quietly tiptoed out of the bedroom, leaving Roman's house.

Chapter Three

Shonda entered the Charlotte Hyatt, carrying her overnight bag on her shoulders and got straight on the elevator headed to the desired room. After one knock the door quickly opened.

"I thought you were bullshitting when I got your text that you were on your way here," Larenzo commented.

"When have you ever known me to bullshit?" Shonda asked, eyeing his shirtless frame.

Larenzo pulled her into his arms, held her, and softly kissed her lips. She slipped her tongue into his mouth and they started kissing passionately. As the temperature between them began to rise, Shonda push at his chest, in an attempt to stop him.

"What…what's wrong?" Larenzo asked, staring into her eyes.

"I have something I want to show you first," she replied.

"Oh, is that so? I have something I wanna show you, too," Larenzo said, grabbing his pulsating shaft.

"I promise it'll be worth the wait," Shonda remarked headed for the suite's bathroom with her belongings in tow.

"Alright don't make me wait too long baby," Larenzo whined.

He kicked off his flipflops, then removed his pajama pants and massaged his semi-hard dick through his briefs. Shonda hurriedly removed the sneakers, leggings, and tee-shirt she'd thrown on, before leaving Roman's house. She showered, afterward she scented her skin, then slipped into the lingerie outfit she'd just worn for Roman. To accentuate the lingerie, she brought along a pair of heels she'd left at Roman's house. She let her shoulder-length brown hair down from the bun it was in, touched her lips with lip gloss, and stared into the mirror. For the extra dramatic effect, she pulled the whip out of her bag and snapped it.

"Perfect." She smiled and exited the bathroom.

Shonda entered the bedroom boldly and confident. The one thing she appreciated when she was with Larenzo was the ability to be free and open. She stood at the end of the bed with her hands on her hips.

Larenzo sat up, his grew wide, and his mouth dropped open. "Goddamn…" he said, getting off the bed walking over to her. He grabbed her hand and spun her around, eyeing all the sexiness she was revealing. "Unh…unh…you sexy as fuck!" Larenzo complimented, licking his lips.

As he pressed his body against Shonda's closing the space between them, his dick throbbed against her backside. Larenzo slipped his hand in her thong and inserted his two fingers inside her opening. Her pussy was on fire and dripping wet. As Larenzo played in and out of her warmth with one hand, he reached down with the other hand and took the whip from her.

"You trying to get real freaky tonight, huh?" Larenzo critiqued.

"Yes," Shonda moaned.

"So, what you want me to do with it?" Larenzo speeded his finger thrusts.

"I…I…unh…want you to tame my wild side." Shonda moaned louder.

"Are you sure about that?" Larenzo looked into her eyes for any sort of hesitation but found none. He was both shocked and intrigued.

"I want you to spank me, Daddy!" She said seductively while nibbling on the side of his neck.

No more words were needed as Larenzo pulled his hand out of her thong and sat down on the edge of the bed.

"You wanna be spanked, baby…I'll spank you…but first, you gotta do something for me." Larenzo rubbed a hand over his beard.

"What?" Shonda asked, easing between his leg, wrapping her arms around his neck, gazing into his eyes. "Anything for you, baby."

"Strip…let see yo' sexy ass dance," Larenzo requested.

Shonda walked over to the dresser and grabbed the remote.

"What are you doing?" Larenzo asked sitting up.

"Have you ever seen a stripper dance without music?" Shonda asked, turning the T.V. on, flipping through the channels until she found the music network. As if the universe knew exactly what they needed for the occasion. *'Feelin' On Your Booty'* by *R. Kelly's* music video played through the screen.

"Now watch me work!" Shonda told Larenzo, standing directly in front of him.

She swayed her hips to the beat of the song, keeping her eyes locked on Larenzo the whole time. She rubbed her hand over her succulent breasts and slowly slid the strap of the lingerie gown off her shoulders one after the other.

Larenzo clapped his hands loudly, "Hell yeah, baby shake that ass!" he cheered.

After dropping the lingerie top, Shonda turned her back to Larenzo. She bent all the way over, touched her ankles, and made her ass clap in Larenzo's face. Shonda looked at Larenzo from between her legs and smiled, while lightly biting her bottom lips.

"Like what you see, Daddy?" Shonda asked.

Larenzo was so turned on, all he could was nod. His dick looked as though it was going to burst through the seam of his briefs.

"I'ma fuck the shit outta of you," Larenzo warned.

"Is that so?" Shonda taunted.

She turned back facing Larenzo, unhooked her thong from the garter leggings, then lifted her foot onto Larenzo's chest, pushing him back down onto the bed.

"Oohhh…shit, my girl bad." Larenzo was thrilled.

Shonda placed a finger over Larenzo's mouth, "Sssshh…this is my show now!"

Larenzo raised his hands, but the grin on his face never vanished. "Whatever you say, Baby." Larenzo relinquished all power over to Shonda.

"Did you bring what I told you too?" Shonda questioned.

Larenzo nodded and pointed to the chair on the other side of the room.

"Yeah, I ain't think you were coming so I left them in the bag," Larenzo informed.

Shonda put her foot back down on the floor. "Don't move." She instructed.

She strutted across the room over to the grey suede chair, against the wall, by the window. She searched around inside Larenzo's bag.

"Oh, it's in the side pocket," Larenzo said.

"Thanks." Shonda reached into each side of his duffle bag until she found what she was looking for. She retrieved the items and headed back over to Larenzo.

"Have you ever used this before?" Shonda asked, tearing open the Trojan vibrating ring.

"Nope, you asked for it, I brought it," Larenzo replied.

Shonda removed the ring from the box, walked over to Larenzo, pulled his briefs down, and took his growing member into her hand. She slid the silicone blue ring on the shaft and pushed it all the way down to the base, slightly above his nuts, then switched it on.

After the ring was secured, Shonda walked over to the side of the bed with the handcuffs.

"Hope you know what you're doing?" Larenzo said, secretly nervous.

He'd never had a woman who at least tried to match his level of freakiness. Shonda's initiative, however, was not only intriguing but a major turn on.

"Don't worry, Larenzo, I'm not gonna hurt you," Shonda assured, kissing his lips. "Now raise your arms over your head."

Larenzo didn't hesitate, he raised both arms over his head, Shonda leaned over, grabbed his wrists, and cuffed them together.

"Not too tight…" Larenzo began, then felt the cuffs lock.

"How's that?" Shonda questioned.

"Fine."

"Good can I continue now?" Shonda asked gazing into his eyes. Larenzo nodded his head. Shonda walked back to the front of Larenzo and began kissing him. She kissed his lips, tonguing him, then moved down to his chest, she sucked on his nipples, while massaging his growing erection.

As Larenzo's dick grew the vibrating ring increased the sensation, making him even harder. Shonda made her way down and took his inches into her mouth. She licked the tip, she could feel the vibrations making his dick swell as it expanded between her jaws.

Larenzo wanted to grab her head and hold it, but unable to, he closed his eyes and shook his foot. "Aahh…fuck!" He groaned loudly.

The vibrations from the ring and Shonda's slippery wet mouth, caused a sensation so strong. He felt his nut rapidly rising and his legs began to tremble, as Shonda took more inches of him into her mouth.

"God…God…damn!" Larenzo raised up off the bed, then fell back. He relented as he let loose deep inside Shonda's throat. Shonda kept sucking until every drop of his thick cum was devoured. "Sss…shit baby that feels so good!" Larenzo moaned.

Shonda released his dick from her mouth, then straddled him. She slid her panties over to the side and eased down onto his tip. As her pussy opened to accommodate his width, she pressed down on his chest. As she slowly began gyrating up and down, she kissed Larenzo.

He pushed his inches deeper inside her, Shonda stopped kissing him and moaned out, as she sped her strokes.

"Uunnhhh…yes…that…f…feels…so…good!" Shonda moaned.

She rode Larenzo up, down, and in circles.

"Fuck me, baby…ride that dick!" Larenzo whispered into her ear, shaking his legs uncontrollably, as the vibrations brought on yet another powerful nut that shot straight up inside her.

As Larenzo's orgasm came to an end, Shonda's began, causing her entire body to tremble, she fell on his chest panting as her orgasm took over.

"I love the time we spend together!" Shonda moaned.

"So…so do I." Larenzo stuttered. "Now that you've satisfied whatever has come over you…" Larenzo and Shonda laughed. "Now it's my turn to have some fun."

"Alright," Shonda agreed as she climbed off Larenzo.

She retrieved the key off the nightstand, next to the bed, and uncuffed him. Larenzo stretched and rolled his wrists to loosen the tension. Then he reached down and switched the vibrating ring off.

After placing the handcuffs and key on the dresser, Shonda walked back over to Larenzo. He grabbed her by the waist and slid her thong down, Shonda kept her heels on, as she pulled her panties completely off. Larenzo pulled her down onto his lap and turned the ring back on. He pressed into her pelvis as he began fucking her rough and hard.

After busting another nut, Larenzo lifted Shonda off his lap and bent her over the bed, on all fours. Larenzo retrieved the whip off the side of the bed and lightly rubbed the strings across her ass.

"Are you sure this is what you want?" Larenzo asked.

"Yes, just be careful not to bruise me too badly," Shonda requested.

Shonda remained in position, as Larenzo smacked her ass with the whip over and over again, careful not to draw blood or bruise her too badly.

"Aahhh…argh…" Shonda screamed as the whip repeatedly came in contact with her cheeks until her legs began to shiver. "Lar…Larenzo…oh…my…God!" Shonda screamed and tears filled her eyes, as the sensations became more powerful and intense than she ever expected.

"Had enough?" Larenzo teased, smacking her ass harder with the whip.

"Aahhh…" Shonda squealed, then nodded.

"Alright," Larenzo agreed, putting the whip down. "Don't move though we ain't finished yet."

Larenzo removed the ring, then entered Shonda from the back. He spent the next few hours, way into the dusk of dawn doing exactly as Shonda requested…*Taming Her Wild Side!*

Chapter Four

Shonda rolled over feeling sore, yet euphoric. She opened her eyes, then sat up in the King size bed. Her eyes scanned around the room until they landed on Larenzo sitting in the chair, smoking a Cuban cigar, with one leg crossed over the other.

"Morning, Sleeping Beauty." He said, through a cloud of smoke.

"Somebody's in a good mood, I see," Shonda commented smiling.

"After last night...well, this morning shall I say. I have good reason to be." Larenzo pulled on the cigar once more. "Daddy's feeling real good today. I could wake up like this every morning."

Shonda stared at him strangely. "I could too except for the fact that..."

Larenzo blew out another cloud of smoke, before cutting her off. "Except that you have a boyfriend. I know...I know."

"Don't look so sad, Larenzo," Shonda stated trying to get out of bed.

She hadn't realized how sore and worn out her body was until she tried to stand up.

"Oooohhh...damn," she groaned.

"Good times last night, huh?" Larenzo boasted.

"Yes, just like every night spent with you," Shonda replied, eyeing him.

Larenzo put out the remainder of the cigar in the tray on the table beside the chair. He got up, walked over to Shonda and grabbed her face with both hands, giving her a deep kiss.

"So, now what?" Larenzo asked.

Shonda rubbed her hands over his shirtless chest. "You can go get some breakfast. I'ma take a bubble bath and try to relax my body."

"You do that, cause I wanna hit that again before we part ways." Larenzo smacked her ass, as she got off the bed.

Shonda turned back to him and smiled, "I was counting on it." She walked over to the table, unplugged her phone from the charger and grabbed her cosmetics bag.

"Guess you won't be seeing ole boy for a while? It's gonna take a couple days to recover from what I did to you last night. Not to mention what I plan to do when I get back." Larenzo arrogantly replied, stroking his chin.

"Shut up and go get my breakfast, so it'll still be hot when I get finished.

Larenzo watched as Shonda sauntered into the bathroom. Once she was finally in the bathroom, he left out to get their breakfast.

After hearing the hotel room door close, she peaked back outside of the bathroom once she confirmed that Larenzo was gone. Shonda pulled up the Pandora app on her phone and let the sounds of *Lyfe Jennings* play, as she cleaned the tub with her own personal cleaning supplies, she never left home without, then turned the water on to run her bath.

After Larenzo returned he and Shonda ate breakfast, then had a couple more rounds of wild, amazing sex. As Larenzo had previously stated, she had to take the rest of the week off to recuperate. She knew Roman would need an explanation, so after she called Nina to give her the rundown for the week, she called Roman.

"Hey, Baby. Are you okay? When I didn't hear from you after you left so abruptly last night. I thought I'd done something wrong," Roman replied immediately after answering his phone.

"No, Roman, I just needed to get back home to finish some contracts for work." Shonda lied. "I'm glad I did, cause I'm not feeling too well, right now."

"Do you want me to come over and take care of you?" Roman offered concerned.

"No, I can take care of myself. I need to get some rest, Roman. I'll call you later, try not to worry too much," Shonda said and hurriedly ended the call.

****

The following Monday, after her brief hiatus, Shonda was ready to get back to work and back to life as usual. She'd taken those days off to relax and think about the conundrum she'd currently gotten herself into. She shook it off and decided to enjoy the ride for as long as she could. As far as she was concerned she had the best of both worlds, there was only one thing that could make things better. But, she knew Roman nor Larenzo would ever go for it, so she quickly pushed the thought out of her mind.

"Damn, I'm glad those whelps are gone," Shonda said, looking in the mirror at her backside, thankful for the strong healing gene in her family. All she had was a few scratches that she figured could easily be explained and justifiable.

When she finally finished getting herself together and arrived at her office, an hour or so later. She was energized and feeling great.

"I see, someone's feeling better," Nina commented as Shonda continued to her office.

"Yeah, I guess you can say that," Shonda responded.

"Well, I'm glad you're feeling better. Your timing is perfect, we have a very busy week ahead of us. Two clients are ready to finalize their offers on properties, and you have an open house today at noon," Nina informed.

"Good, thanks for holding shit down, while I was gone, Nina. I don't know what I'd do without you." Shonda walked around and sat down in her desk chair.

"This is my business, too. Besides, you would've done the same thing for me," Nina replied.

Once Shonda got settled into her office and updated her iPhone with the viewings for the week, she was ready to head out to take care of business. After filing paperwork, sealing the deals on two houses that morning. Shonda headed straight to her open house. She was excited that a new client was interested in doing business with her. When she arrived at the property, she didn't see any cars parked in the driveway or on the street nearby.

A strange feeling quickly rushed her. "What the hell is going on here?" She asked out loud, still scanning the area.

She finally decided to get out and wait inside for her client. About ten minutes after entering the house there was a knock at the door.

"Are you serious, right now?" Shonda hissed after opening the door. "I know damn well you're not the new client I'm supposed to be meeting?" she fumed.

"Well, I figured this would be the only way to get the answers I'm searching for out of you," Roman replied pushing his way past her into the house.

Shonda slammed the door shut and turned facing him, hands on her hips, and a grimace on her face.

"Roman I can't have you popping up in the middle of my work day like this," Shonda snapped.

"You leave me in the middle of the night, don't answer my calls or texts, then go M.I.A. for over a week, but you got the nerve to be pissed at me?" Roman chuckled. "Women ain't never fucking satisfied."

"Roman, I told you I was si…" Shonda started but was cut off by the raise of Roman's hand.

"Shonda were you really sick or was you fucking around. And don't lie, I've noticed the changes in you over the past few months. First, you started complaining about little shit, then bringing up the fifty shades of grey freaky bullshit. Now you doing disappearing acts with no explanation," Roman stated with an accusing tone and glare.

Shonda didn't want to lie to Roman, but there was no way she could admit the truth either.

She exhaled deeply, shook her head, and smirked. "Roman, just because I need space doesn't mean you get to come to my place of business and accuse me of fuckin' around," Shonda snapped.

Roman eyed Shonda sternly, "Are you? It's a simple yes or no, Shonda," he barked.

'Fuck what am I going to do?' Shonda asked herself as thoughts stormed her brain. Then it hit her, the one thing that always calmed Roman down and shut him up no matter where they were. She closed the space between them, grabbed Roman's belt and started unbuckling it.

"What are you doing?" Roman asked shooting his eyes down at her.

"Shush," Shonda ordered and went back to undoing his belt and slacks.

She slipped them down past his knees and freed his inches from the slit in his briefs. She started slowly massaging his flesh with her hands. After three slow, steady strokes he was rock hard. Shonda licked around the tip slowly causing his leg to shake.

"St...stop...shit!" Roman moaned as she took the whole tip into her mouth and teased it with her tongue ring. "D...da...damn, Baby!" Roman fell back against the door, closed his eyes, and grabbed the back of her head. He pushed more of his inches into her mouth, as she speeded her sucking. "Aaah...sss...shit, baby suck that dick!" Roman moaned.

He thrust his dick in and out, and in a circular motion until he was touching the back of her throat. Minutes later, Roman released inside Shonda's mouth, she swallowed and got up off the floor. Before she could say anything, Roman picked her up and carried her through the empty house. He entered the kitchen and laid her down on top of the granite island counter. Roman started kissing Shonda and caressing her breasts at the same time.

"Uumm..." Shonda moaned.

Roman eased his hands up her skirt, raised it halfway, and moved her panties over to the side. His pants were still down, his dick was growing hard all over again. He placed his throbbing tip at the slit of her opening. He rubbed it up and down, until she was soaking wet, then entered her. Roman pressed down on the counter, pushed his inches inside her, and started stroking her hard and fast.

Shonda put her legs up on his shoulders and laid all the way back for more leverage. "Ooohh…shit, Baby!" she moaned

"Yeah, you like that huh? Want me to go harder?" Roman asked.

Shonda nodded unable to speak as the pressure of his thrusts got harder and quicker.

"Nah, answer me, this what you want right?" Roman pushed even deeper inside her.

"Ro…Roman…baby…it…it…" Shonda cried out.

"It's what?" Roman glared into her eyes menacingly. "This pussy belongs to me, Shonda!" He growled fucking her even harder.

"Ooohh…shit…you're hur…hurtin'…me!" Tears filled Shonda's eyes.

This was a side of Roman she had never experienced before. At first, she started enjoying it, but now it felt like Roman was attacking her. She tried to put her legs down to release some of the pressure. Roman grabbed her legs holding them in the crease of his arms, and held them open, fucking her harder.

"You wanted this dick rough and hard. So, you getting it rough and hard today." Roman gritted through clenched teeth.

Shonda was ready for his assault to be over. She grabbed the back of his neck with her hands, started squeezing her walls, and kissing him at the same time, in hopes of making him nut.

"Oh, yeah, you think you slick!" Roman teased breaking their kiss. "You can squeeze them walls all you want. I jacked off before I got here, and with the nut, I released from that bomb ass head. I can go for at least

another hour. Matter of fact get up and turn around."
Roman pulled his dick out and stared at Shonda.

"Roman, I'm sore and tired," Shonda whined.

"I don't give a fuck…turn that ass around now!"
Roman commanded.

Shonda saw the seriousness in his eyes, as she turned
her back to him, her legs trembled.

"Get up on the counter, on your knees," Roman
instructed stroking his dick back to its full capacity.

Shonda stepped out of her shoes and dropped her skirt
and panties. As she climbed on top of the counter her body
shook. Roman anxious to get back to attacking her pussy,
grabbed her waist and helped her onto the counter. He
grabbed the back of her neck and pushed her forward.

"Arch your back," he instructed. "Raise your ass in the
air and spread your legs wide."

Shonda did as she was told in hopes of this ending
soon. She closed her eyes afraid of what was going to
happen next. Before her mind had the chance to wander
too far, she felt something wet pouring down the crack of
her ass. She opened her eyes and peeked behind her and
caught Roman spitting in his hand, massaging it on his dick,
which meant he'd also spit in her ass as well.

"Roman, please baby, I have to go back to work!"
Shonda pleaded.

"Tell me the truth. Are you fucking another nigga?"
Roman asked still stroking his dick.

"Baby…I love you, Roman! I love you and only you. I
just wanted to spice things up that's all," Shonda pleaded
convincingly.

"Well, you're about to get what you wished for. Then
you're bringing your ass home with me."

"Roman, I can't right now," Shonda declined.

Roman was silent and Shonda wondered why he wasn't saying anything. Until she felt her ass being stretched open by his two fingers.

"Uunnh…" she moaned and squirmed trying to ease the pain.

"You coming home with me?" Roman asked pushing another finger, making it three inside of her asshole.

"Uuunnnh…Ro…Roman…sto…stop, Baby!" Shonda begged.

"Nah!" Roman shook his head and replaced his fingers with his tip at the center of her ass. He mounted her like a raging bull and entered her asshole forcibly.

"Aaahhh!" Shonda screamed, biting down on her bottom lip.

"This the kinda spice you want?" Roman asked clutching her shoulders, fucking her hard.

"Ro…Ro…"

"Come home!" Roman ordered.

He removed his hands from her shoulders and slid one in front of her. He found her clit and started rubbing two fingers over it back and forth until it was protruding.

Shonda's body shook uncontrollably, and her juices started squirting. "Oohhh…sss…shit…Roman! That feels so…so…so good!" She squealed as tears fell from her face.

"I love you, Shonda. I need you home, Baby!" He said, pulling his dick out of her.

He lifted her up in his arms, turned her around, and reentered her pussy this time more gently. He kissed the tears still falling from her eyes, as he made love to her and turned back into the sensitive Roman she was used too.

"See baby I can fuck you all day if that's what you want, but I'd rather make love to you!" He kissed her passionately and they both came simultaneously.

"Ta…take me home, Baby!" Shonda said in barely a whisper once they were finished.

She was so exhausted she could barely move, let alone walk.

"Are you sure, what about your car?" Roman asked.

"I'll get it tomorrow. I just want to go home and make love to you until I can't anymore, then fall asleep."

"Alright, your wish is my command."

Roman smiled as he lifted her in his arms, she threw her arms around his neck and rested her head on his chest. His mission had been accomplished. He'd come there with every intention of dragging her back home with him if need be but knowing all it took to make her comply was a couple of rough, deep strokes had him on cloud nine.

Chapter Five

Shonda looked down at Roman who was knocked out sleeping with his arm laid across her stomach. She slowly sat up and eased from under him. Then got out of bed and headed to the bathroom. Still naked from the night before she stood in the mirror admiring Roman's handy work. She was covered in hickies from her neck all the way down to her thighs.

She blushed hard, "What the fuck got into him?" she asked.

She pulled the shower curtain back and cut on the hot water. She didn't realize how sore she was until she stepped in the shower, and the hot water poured. As the water cascaded down on her, she closed her eyes, and let her mind wander. She thought about what had transpired between her and Roman and questioned if it was just a tactic to get her to come back to his house.

She also thought about the other man who'd been rocking her world. But, how would she get away from Roman to have another rendezvous with Larenzo? She'd promised Roman she would never leave him again during their marathon lovemaking.

After showering, Shonda dressed and left for work. She'd turned her phone off when she and Roman returned to his house the previous afternoon. So, when she got in the car she turned it back on. She'd missed three calls and voice messages from Nina. Two text messages from Larenzo, and one voice message.

She didn't bother calling Nina back, she'd see her once she got to the office. She and Nina had not only been roommates all through college and shortly after until she moved out. They had also opened a successful real estate business together that has been thriving since 2009, eight years and counting.

She replied to a client's text, then opened Larenzo's messages. The first one was a picture with a caption, she opened the picture and her pussy jumped instantly.

She read the caption: //: *Hope this motivates you to hurry up and come give Daddy what he needs!*

Shonda was floored, Larenzo's naked body and curved inches had her so excited she could feel her pussy juices oozing into her panties. She closed her legs and opened the other message, which only made her even more turned on. It was a video this time, she pressed play and watched in awe. Although Larenzo said nothing in the video, his actions told her everything she needed to know.

****

"What the hell happened to you?" Nina scolded the minute Shonda entered the office.

"Girrrllll…" Shonda shrieked as she strolled into her office.

Nina followed her and shut the door behind them. "Um, I'm waiting for an explanation, Missy. One minute you're leaving to go show an open house to a new client. Next thing I know you don't return to work, or answer any of my calls. Then you stroll in here this morning like nothing happened. What gives Shonda?" Nina was unamused by the smile on Shonda's face.

"Well, something did happen, alright! I think my man finally got the hint. He was the client at the open house…"

46

"Roman was the person you showed the open house too?" Nina was shocked.

"Yes, he was pissed that I left him the night before my week-long hiatus. So, he felt that was the only way…"

"So, what happened?" Nina asked intrigued.

"I can tell you if you stop cutting me off. Anyway, we argued for a few minutes about him manipulating my work schedule. Then he accused me of cheating and wouldn't let the situation go…" Shonda paused at Nina's raised finger. "What?" she questioned.

"Are you cheating? Cause you have been different lately," Nina reminded. "I was wondering if it was because of another man."

"I'll tell you because I know you'll keep your mouth shut. Yes, I've been seeing someone else for a couple months. But it was just for the sex, to fill the void I was missing with Roman. But, after this weekend, I'm conflicted. The only reason I started fucking Larenzo…"

"*Larenzo!* Wait isn't that Roman's…"

"Yes…yes, it is now you see why you can't let this conversation leave this office."

"Got you, back to you and Roman."

"Anyway, so as he was accusing me of cheating. I had to drop to my knees and give him some bomb ass head to shut him the fuck up. Then he took me into the kitchen and sat me down on the counter…" Shonda paused as shivers rushed through her, the thoughts had her hot and bothered again. "To make a long story short, he fucked the shit outta me right there on the counter. Then we went home and fucked more as he begged me not to leave him. Roman has never made me cum as much as he did in the past twenty-four hours. Hell, my pussy and ass still sore. I'm surprised I'm able to walk.

Nina sat there eyeing Shonda with her mouth open. "Well, damn guess you really have been a busy little grasshopper."

"You have no idea. Roman made me promise not to leave him or give his pussy away. He said he will fuck me anyway I want from now on. I knew he had it in him. Like I told you, I love Roman, I just needed more sexually."

"So, let me ask you this if you had to choose between Roman or Larenzo who would you pick? You do know you can't have them both, right? Just for moral reasons alone," Nina stated.

"I know Nina, I love Roman. We've been together almost three years, but I know what to expect with Roman…well at least I used to. With Larenzo, each time we're together it's a mystery. I never know what that man is going to do. They're both hung like horses, but Larenzo finesses my pussy in ways I never knew was possible."

"Well sounds like you have a problem, boo. If you're not careful this shit could backfire fast and you don't wanna be responsible for the aftermath that can ensue."

"Nina, what's the worst that can happen?"

"How about you getting hurt by one of them or one of them hurting each other? Does Larenzo even know about you and Roman?" Nina scratched her head confused by the whole situation.

"He knows I have a man, but I never mentioned his name. Whereas Roman, on the other hand, thinks I'm his one and only," Shonda replied, not feeling any remorse about her current actions.

"Well, you better hope Larenzo doesn't find out the truth and that Roman keeps thinking you're his one and only!" Nina warned.

"Nina, I know what I'm doing," Shonda insisted.

"If you say so just be careful Shonda, you're treading on very thin ice."

"I'll keep that in mind, Nina."

Nina got up to head back to her office, but stopped, and turned back facing Shonda. "One last question, whose dick is better Roman or Larenzo?"

"If you would have asked me that before last night definitely Larenzo. Now I'm not so sure. I'm gonna have to go fuck Larenzo now to compare skills," Shonda giggled.

"You so crazy, but don't worry, my lips are sealed. Just keep me posted on how things turn out."

"I will, thanks again, Nina."

"Anytime."

****

//: *Need you home asap…it's an emergency!*

Once lunch rolled around she received a text from Roman, so she rushed home. When she arrived, she noticed her car parked in its usual spot. She parked Roman's truck next to her car and hurried inside the house.

"Roman!" Shonda yelled. "Roman where…"

"I'm in the living room!" Roman called out.

"What's so important I had to rush ho…" Shonda stopped mid-sentence, dropped her purse, keys, and mouth all at the same time.

"We couldn't go another minute without you." Roman smiled, standing in the middle of the living room floor, butt naked, stroking his iron hard steel.

"Really?" Shonda replied seductively.

She hurried over to him, wrapped her arms around his neck, and kissed him. "I think I can take care of that," She said after breaking the kiss.

"You sure about that? Cause I don't want you out of commission when you go back to work." Roman joked caressing her ass.

"I won't be, you're the one who should be worried Mr. *I had to take a day off work to recover,*" Shonda teased.

"Yeah, well I'm all rested up now. So, we'll see who has the last laugh."

"Sounds like a challenge, hope you can keep up," Shonda said arrogantly.

"Oh, trust I can." Roman boasted confidently.

Shonda tightly grabbed his chin and gazed into his eyes. "I can show you better than I can tell you." She pushed Roman down on the couch.

"Oh, shit that's what I'm talking about," Roman said grinning like a Cheshire cat.

Shonda walked over to him and slapped his face.

"What the fuck?" Roman grabbed his face, stunned.

"Shut the fuck up! This is my show," Shonda commanded. "Do I make myself clear?"

Roman nodded, while Shonda still held his face. "Yes, ma'am!"

"Good, now put your hands behind your head and keep your eyes on me," Shonda instructed.

Roman did as he was told, he put his hands behind his head, and kept his eyes locked on Shonda, while she slowly began stripping out of her work clothes.

"Um…um, my baby sexy as hell." Roman complimented once she was completely naked.

Shonda strolled over to the couch, climbed on Roman's lap, and straddled him. She held the back of his head and started kissing him. As their tongues wrestled, Shonda slightly lifted up, positioned Roman's tip at her center, and slid down a little until the head and just a few inches of shaft was inside her.

Roman cupped her ass and spread it open for more leverage as he pushed more inches inside her walls.

"Unh…unh damn you feel so good!" Roman groaned. "That pussy wet as hell."

"You like this pussy?" Shonda moaned into his ear.

"Aahhh…shit…hell yeah!" Roman replied as Shonda applied more pressure and speed to her strokes.

Shonda tightly held the back of Roman's neck, raised up onto her feet in a kneeling position, arched her back, and stroked Roman in a circular motion.

"Ooohh…sss…baby! You're driving me, crazy woman!" Roman moaned closing his eyes, biting his bottom lip.

Shonda released the hold on his neck, paused her stroke and leaned back. She pressed her hands flat onto the floor and repositioned her legs straight out, over Roman's shoulders, then commenced to giving him hard, quick, rotated thrusts. She rotated on his dick round and round until her walls swallowed every inch.

Roman threw his head back on the couch. "Ride that dick baby, give me all of that pussy!" he moaned.

"Roman your dick's so big and hard. Fuck me, baby…fuck me please!" Shonda screamed as an orgasm surfaced.

Roman grabbed her waist and fucked her even harder. Her body started trembling and she pressed firmer onto the floor to maintain her balance, as she exploded and creamed all over his dick. Before she could catch her breath, Roman lifted her off the floor. He stood up with her straddled around his waist, and his dick still deep inside her. He held onto her, walked her over to the nearest wall, and began pounding. When Shonda tried to move he stopped her.

"Nah, it's my turn stay still and take this dick," Roman instructed, kissing her lips.

"Whatever, you say baby!" Shonda moaned breaking their kiss.

She rested her back and head against the wall and allowed Roman to take over. He pounded her slow, fast, fast and hard, until he finally let loose and nutted.

"God, I love you!" Roman moaned breathlessly, nibbling on her earlobe.

"I love you, too!" Shonda panted, as he pulled out and let her back onto the floor. "Now I have to shower and get back to work. Thanks, for getting my car."

"It was no biggie just a simple cab ride. Are you sure you can't stay longer?" Roman begged.

"Roman I gotta get back to work. It'll be more of this when I get off tonight…promise." Shonda cupped his face and kissed him passionately. "I am loving this new side of you."

"I'm loving it too, now get upstairs before you start something you can't finish."

"Oh, I can finish that's never a problem, save all that shit talking for tonight."

When Shonda finished showering and changing, as she came back downstairs an eerie feeling rushed over her, especially when Roman met her in the foyer with her purse and keys dangling from each hand.

He leaned in and kissed her on the cheek, "Enjoy the rest of your day, Baby. I'll see you later," Roman said.

Shonda felt it was more of a question than a statement, so she simply nodded, grabbed her things, and headed out the door.

CHASTITY ADAMS

Chapter Six

Two Days Later…

Roman entered Starbucks and scanned the room until he found who he was there to see. He walked over to the table and sat in the chair across from his guest.

"Well…well, this is a funny turn of events." The guest stated sarcastically.

"Well, you need something from me and I need something from you. So, can we get on with it?" Roman stated with a frown.

"Roman, you already know if I never see your ass again it'll be too soon. Don't get it twisted my intentions here are strictly business," Larenzo replied.

"Okay, let's get on with it. I'd rather be anywhere but here," Roman sighed heavily.

Larenzo slid a manila folder over to Roman and kept his eyes locked on his facial expressions.

"Just save me the time of reading through all this and tell me what you need," Roman requested.

"I'm expanding the business and even though your ass don't do shit. That still doesn't change the fact, that pops left the company to both of us. So, I can't make any moves without both of our signatures on those documents," Larenzo informed.

"Oh, right and I'm supposed to give you my half of the company just like that?" Roman fussed.

"Fuck you, nigga. Don't flip this shit on me. You decided being part of Pierce Construction wasn't good enough for you. You turned your back on the family to become some rich, architect sell out," Larenzo argued.

"Yes, I did and I ain't apologizing for wanting more outta my life. But, from the looks of these documents, you seem to be doing well with the company. Pops would be proud," Roman complimented easing his tone.

"Wow, did Roman Pierce just compliment somebody?" Larenzo asked sarcastically.

"Shut up, nigga, but um before I sign these papers. I have a few more questions I need answered." Roman closed the folder and pulled his phone from his pants pocket.

"What else do you need to know, everything is plain in white and black?" Larenzo replied.

Roman opened his phone, pulled up his latest picture of Shonda dressed in one of her work outfits, smiling innocently, and slid the phone over to Larenzo.

Larenzo picked the phone up and it didn't take for him to recognize the person in the picture. Roman watched as Larenzo's smile faded and his brows creased.

"What's wrong, Renzo?" Roman asked not taking his eyes off Larenzo.

"What the fuck you doing with my bitch muthafucker," Larenzo snapped, raising his voice.

"First of all, calm the fuck down. Secondly, watch who you calling a bitch. And lastly what the fuck are you talking about?" Roman answered, now also creasing his brows.

"Fuck you and these muthafuckers in here! Tell me why you got a picture of my woman in your phone?" Larenzo continued his tone getting angrier.

"Renzo, I don't know what you're smokin' but this is *my* woman." Roman asserted.

"Oh really, you sure about that..." Larenzo pulled out his phone.

He went to his photos and pulled up a picture Shonda she's sent him one day during her hiatus. She was dressed in a purple lingerie outfit, making a seductive kissy face. Larenzo slid the phone over to Roman. When Roman picked it up he couldn't believe what he was seeing. He stared at the picture fighting the rage brewing inside him and repeatedly shook his head.

"Nah…it can't be…" Roman fumed.

"It is, so how do you know, Shonda?" Larenzo persisted.

"I've been dating her for damn near eight months. The better question is…*how do you know, Shonda?*

"I met her at bike fest in Myrtle Beach over the summer," Larenzo responded, trying to process everything that had transpired since he met Shonda.

"I didn't know you went to Bike Fest?" Roman shrugged.

"Every year…" Larenzo nodded, taking a sip of his frappe to calm his nerves.

"She didn't tell you she had a man?" Roman wondered unable to take her eyes off the picture on Larenzo's phone.

"She did, but she said it wasn't serious," Larenzo played back all the lies Shonda had obviously told him. "Roman, I never would've fucked wit' her if I knew."

"I know, but Shonda knew, which means she did this shit on purpose!" Roman snapped.

Larenzo shook his head, then started laughing.

"What the fuck's so funny?" Roman asked.

"After all these years, it figures it would take us fucking the same girl to bring us back together. It's just like old times," Larenzo admitted.

"Yep and like old times, I think we should flip the switch on that lying, cheating ass, bitch," Roman suggested.

"You mean like back in the day before you stopped being my right-hand man?" Larenzo asked.

"Exactly, we can go back to hating each other later. We can't let Shonda get away with playing us like suckas." Roman nodded.

"So, what you got in mind, Ro-Ro?" Larenzo stated down for whatever Roman, had in store. "Looks like Ro-Ro and Renzo are back at it."

"Let the games begin!" Roman agreed.

He and Larenzo shook hands, he signed the documents in the folder, then they discussed their plans to get back at Shonda.

****

A Week Later...

"So, everything's going well with you and Roman I assume?" Nina asked Shonda as they left the office headed to the parking lot.

"I have that man eating out of the palm of my hand. He even said he has a surprise for me for my birthday." Shonda replied.

"Oh, okay. So, you still going to the erotic book convention in South Carolina this weekend?"

Shonda nodded, "Yep, I'm leaving tonight I have a pit stop to make first," she blushed.

"Oh Lord, you're going to see Larenzo aren't you?" Nina's tone was filled with disappointment.

58

"I gotta get one last hurrah before Roman tries to tie me down for good. I honestly think that's what he's leading toward."

"Like I said you better hope this doesn't blow up in your face, because a lot of people can get hurt if it does."

"Nina, what Roman doesn't know can't hurt anybody. I'm not worried about Larenzo he knows the deal already."

"And there's no possibility that Roman knows your dirty secret or that Larenzo's feelings for you haven't escalated?"

"Not to my knowledge. Nina, you worry too much. I have it all under control, after this weekend, I'll be done with Larenzo. Because I told you, I love, Roman!"

"Good, be careful this weekend and have fun."

"I will Nina."

****

Shonda pulled up to the Pierce Construction site, she parked next to Larenzo's midnight blue Ford truck. She walked over to the trailer, as she raised her fist to knock on the door it popped opened and Larenzo's smiling face appeared.

"Well, someone's happy to see me." Shonda beamed.

"Damn right, get that ass in here." Larenzo grabbed her hand, pulling her into him.

He closed the trailer door behind them and they started tonguing one another. As they kissed Larenzo eased his hands up underneath the denim skirt she was wearing and slid her panties down. Shonda could feel his dick coming to life through his blue construction jumpsuit. She reached down and started massaging it through the fabric.

"Damn, I missed you." Larenzo breathed into her ear.

He removed the remainder of her clothes then stepped back and let his construction jumpsuit down to the floor.

"I missed you, too," Shonda replied she slid Larenzo's briefs down to his ankles, freeing his wood.

Larenzo kicked his shoes off, along with his jumpsuit, and boxers. Larenzo stood over her making sure there was no extra space between them.

"What are you doing?" Shonda asked nervously.

"Just stay still woman. I got you," Larenzo promised. "Close your eyes and relax," he instructed.

"What are you going to do Larenzo?" Shonda looked at him sternly.

"You'll like it, I promise," Larenzo assured, kissing her once more to calm her nerves.

"Okay, I trust you but…"

"No buts Shonda." Larenzo placed his finger over her mouth shushing her.

Larenzo eased behind Shonda, reached down and scooped her off her feet with one arm. Holding her securely in the creases of his arms, he walked backward and rested against the wall. Larenzo flipped her upside down and held her legs so that her pussy was in his face.

Shonda could feel the blood rushing to her head as she opened her eyes and realized she was hanging upside down.

"Larenz…" she started, but quickly paused when she felt Larenzo's tongue part her opening.

As Larenzo's tongue-lashing became increasingly intense she grabbed ahold of Larenzo's legs and held tight. She started feeling more pleasure, than fear, Shonda positioned her head and put his dick in her mouth.

Larenzo nibbled her clit and licked her slit, Shonda sucked and licked his length. She was in the zone until her legs quivered and an orgasm rushed her. She let Larenzo's dick fall out of her mouth and gasped with pleasure.

"Sh…shit…L…Larenzo!" Shonda squealed as her orgasm came full force. "Uunnh…aahhh…it feels so…good."

Larenzo nibbled her clit harder and flicked his tongue until Shonda's leg clasped around his neck. He continued licking until she finally relaxed and released her hold on his neck.

"Damn, baby, guess you liked that?" Larenzo taunted with a slight giggle.

Shonda couldn't speak, she just nodded and exhaled.

"Okay, now you can finish what you started," Larenzo said.

Shonda didn't need to ask what he meant. She opened her mouth and took his semi-swollen member back into her throat. She licked and sucked until Larenzo released and pulled out.

"Can you put me down now? I think I'm getting dizzy and I still have to drive later," Shonda requested.

Larenzo reached down and lifted her up, then turned her facing him. He cradled her into the creases of his arms and held her around his waist. Shonda threw her arms around his neck and raised up, so he could place his dick at the center, then she came down on it until half of his inches were buried inside her.

"Aw shit ride that dick, baby." Larenzo moaned pushing more inches inside her walls. "This dick feels good don't it?"

"Uh huh." Shonda nodded, swaying her hips harder. "Yes, that dick feels so fucking good."

Larenzo cupped her ass in each hand and spread open her cheeks giving her more inches as he pushed inside her hard and ferociously.

"Larenzo, oh God fuck me!" Shonda screamed. "You're driving me…aahh…sss…shit." Shonda kissed Larenzo and worked her hips in a circular motion.

As her hips speeded, his strokes increased. They erupted together and remained in the moment until they were able to speak again. Larenzo finally let Shonda down onto the floor.

"I have a shower in the back if you want to use it," Larenzo offered.

"Hell no, I'm not using a shower that a bunch of guys rotate in and out of. I'll shower when I get to the hotel." Shonda refused.

"Are you sure you'll be able to drive after all that?" Larenzo questioned worriedly.

"I'll be fine, Larenzo. I'll call and let you know I made it safely, but please don't get clingy and overprotective." Shonda eyed him, then kissed him on the lips one final time.

"Can you blame a brother for not being able to get enough of his girlfriend?" Larenzo replied he threw girlfriend in to see what her reaction would be.

"Girlfriend, I didn't know we'd made that official yet," Shonda replied, eyeing him strangely.

"Look I know you have a man, but you said the shit wasn't serious. I think it's 'bout time we do something about that," Larenzo said, grabbing ahold of her chin, staring deep into her eyes. "I'm falling in love with you

Shonda and I can't fathom the idea of sharing you with another man," he replied.

Shonda's heart dropped and she slowly backed away from him. "Larenzo, I'm flattered, but I better get out of here before it gets too late."

"Okay, guess I'll talk to you later?" Larenzo gloomily replied.

"I promise you will. Bye Larenzo, it's been fun."
Shonda eased out of the trailer more confused than before.

Chapter Seven

Shonda sat at her desk, going over recent transactions for the month. She was busy calculating numbers on the college standard calculator when a text from Roman interrupted her.

9-9-2017…1:17 P.M.

//: Can't wait to see you tomorrow. Prepare yourself for one hell of a birthday surprise! ~Roman~

//: Already prepared, just wish you'd tell me what it is. The suspense is killing me! ~Shonda~

//: Don't worry, you're gonna love it! ~Roman~

//: I'll be the judge of that! ☺ ~Shonda~

//: Don't let your mouth write a check, your ass can't cash! Lmao! ~Roman~ ☺

Shonda blushed reading Roman's last text.

"Somebody's happy," Nina commented standing in Shonda's office doorway.

"Roman has a surprise for me tomorrow," Shonda responded with a wide grin.

Nina entered the office and sat in the chair in front of Shonda's desk.

"Well, you deserve it birthday girl," Nina stated.

"What can I say, Roman's full of surprises these days," Shonda remarked still smiling.

Nina crossed her legs, eyeing Shonda. "So, have you ended that other situation yet?"

Shonda's smile suddenly vanished. "I haven't spoken to Larenzo in weeks. It's safe to say that chapter is closed," Shonda answered with hope. "Now I can focus my attention on the future with Roman."

"Damn, girl you dodged a bullet. Not many women can do what you did and still live to tell about it," Nina shook her head in disbelief.

"I know and after Roman already accused me of cheating. I can't give him any more reason to doubt my love or loyalty," Shonda confessed remorseful.

"I hope everything works out for you and Roman," Nina responded. "But, you never told me how you ended up in the situation with Larenzo in the first place."

"It was during Bike Fest on Memorial Day weekend," Shonda started explaining.

"Oh, yeah, I remember you going down there." Nina nodded.

"Yeah, well I asked Roman to go but he was too busy. So, I went by myself, the day of the Fest I was enjoying the sites and whatnot so to speak. When I ran into Larenzo, we chatted a little while about Roman and his whereabouts. He told me I shouldn't be out there by myself, so we spent the entire day together. Later that night we were tipsy, one thing led to another. I ended up having the best sex I'd ever had round after round. I'm talking all night into the wee hours of the morning marathon sex..." Shonda crossed her legs as the thought of what Larenzo did to her caused tingles to shoot through her pussy. "Anyway, to make a long story short, we promised that night would be the only night, but I couldn't stop craving the euphoria he made me feel," Shonda continued.

"So, you kept fucking him and now just like that you can let go and never look back?" Nina asked unconvinced.

"I never said I could, but I have too. Cause if I don't I will lose Roman and all that we've been to one another." Shonda answered.

"What if the truth about you and Larenzo comes out? You'll still lose everything you and Roman built. So, please be careful," Nina warned.

"I will, Nina," Shonda replied.

After work, Shonda rushed home, showered, packed her bags, and relaxed for the night. The next morning, at 8:35 a.m. Shonda boarded a plane headed to Atlantic City. She was anxious, she hadn't seen Roman in over a week. She was also anxious to know what the secret surprise was. She spent the majority of the flight pondering what she would say if he popped the question. She coached herself to be patient and keep an open mind. All she knew for sure was that her body craved to be touched and her hand itched at the thought of all the money she planned to win at Atlantic City's many casinos.

****

Roman and Larenzo took turns bench pressing inside the hotel's gym. While discussing their agenda.

"She has no idea what this weekend is about, right?" Larenzo asked finishing his sets.

"No, she thinks it's just to celebrate her birthday," Roman answered, switching places with him, laying down on the bench press seat. "So, how'd she react when you said those words?"

"Oh, you mean when I told her, I loved her?" Larenzo chuckled. "She couldn't get away from me fast enough."

"Good, she has no clue we're on to her lying, cheating ass and that's exactly how we want it," Roman replied, finishing his set, then getting up. "Well, if you don't mind I gotta go shower so I can meet our guest of honor at the airport."

"Alright, text me when it's showtime," Larenzo said returning to the bench.

As soon as Shonda arrived at Atlantic City's International Airport, she headed straight for luggage claim. Just as she was about to reach to get her suitcase, she felt someone behind her, then his voice boomed in her ear.

"Let me help with that little mama?" he said.

"I got it, besides my boyfriend wouldn't be happy about that," Shonda remarked.

Roman pressed closer against her, closing the space between them, making sure she could feel his growing hard-on against her ass. She wiggled her ass on his dick, feeling her pussy get hot and wet.

"Keep that up we gonna have to make a pit stop before we get to the hotel," Roman whispered.

"Stop playing and let's get out of here," Shonda said.

"So damn bossy…" Roman commented grabbing Shonda's bag, following behind her out of the airport exit doors.

"You happy to be in Atlantic City for your birthday?" Roman asked throwing her luggage into the popped trunk.

"Yes, I'm definitely anxious to see what you have planned for me this weekend."

Roman smirked, "Trust me you will not be disappointed."

As they arrived at the hotel, Roman and Shonda walked hand in hand, past the receptionist desk, straight to heavily guarded elevators. When they entered the Marina suite Shonda took in the scenery. Everything from the massive living room and the even bigger bedroom, with a beautiful view of the Marina Bay from every window.

Roman sat Shonda's bag down on the plush king size bed. Shonda sat down on the leather sectional couch and removed her earrings and shoes.

"I'm jumping in the shower. Wanna join me?" Shonda asked, removing her top and stepping out of her tights.

"Don't tempt me...get yo' ass in that shower before we miss breakfast altogether," Roman said, smacking her ass hard.

"Now who's tempting who?" Shonda asked grabbing his dick, squeezing it hard.

"Aahhh what the hell, we can be a little late," Roman said, biting his bottom lip.

Roman grabbed Shonda by the waist, pushing his steel into her backside, as he guided her into the bathroom. Once they were in the bathroom, Roman shut the door, then Shonda slammed him against it, and yanked his shirt out of his pants revealing his abs. Shonda rubbed her hand along his abs, as fire surged through their veins. Shonda grabbed the back of Roman's neck and hungrily kissed him while slipping her tongue into his mouth. Roman slid Shonda's panties down, then fumbled to undo her bra.

Shonda broke their kiss, backed away from Roman, and removed her bra, as he quickly came out of his shoes and clothes. Shonda turned the hot water on, then the cold water and lastly the shower. Once the water was to her liking, she stepped in, pulling Roman by the hand behind her.

Roman wasted no time, lifting her leg onto the side of the tub and sliding his inches halfway inside her slippery wetness. Shonda wrapped her hands behind Roman's neck and rested her head on his shoulders, as his thrusts got harder and her breathing escalated.

"Goo…God, I missed you." Roman said into her ear while nibbling on her lobe.

"Me too…now less talking…more…fu…fuck…fucking!" Shonda begged.

Roman clutched Shonda's waist pushing all his inches inside her and pounded into her hard and quick.

"Aaahhh…Ro…Roman…" Shonda moaned loudly.

"Yeah…make me cum baby!"

Shonda swayed her hips to his rhythm and as he requested she made him cum, at the exact same time an orgasm rushed through her and oozed out. They stayed intertwined as the water from the shower cascaded down onto them. Before Roman could pull out, his dick grew hard again. Shonda maneuvered until his dick plopped out of her.

"W…what you doing?" Roman murmured.

Shonda placed her finger over his lips. She turned facing him. "Lift my leg," she commanded.

Roman lifted her right leg into the crease of his arms and Shonda grabbed his tip and guided it back to her center. Shonda held onto Roman's shoulders and threw her hips, as he speeded his strokes and their mouths join together. They open their mouths simultaneously and their tongues danced.

"You feel so fucking good." Shonda squealed.

"So, do you...baby..." Roman agreed, biting then sucking the left side of her neck.

****

Shonda and Roman finished showering and got dressed, then headed to the restaurant for brunch. After ordering their food, Roman slid an envelope over to Shonda.

"What's this?" Shonda asked, picking up the envelope.

"Open it and find out," Roman said, smiling.

Shonda opened the envelope and inside there was an appointment slip to the hotel's salon and spa an hour from the current time.

"Roman, you didn't have to do this," Shonda said, smiling as she read all the amenities her appointment offered.

"It's your birthday baby, I wanted to go all out," Roman said. "This way you can get your nails done, your hair, get waxed, facials, massages and all that shit all at once." Roman shrugged. "It just sounded like a good deal to me."

"It's a great deal, thank you!" Shonda shrieked happily, getting up from her chair, leaning over planting a kiss on his lips.

After the waitress brought their food back over to the table, Shonda wasted no time satisfying her hunger.

"Where will you be while I'm getting all this done?" Shonda asked Roman as he pulled out his wallet to pay the ticket.

"At the bar watching T.V. and drinking probably. Or I might try my luck at the casino for a while," Roman replied.

"Okay, have fun and I will see soon," Shonda said.

"Enjoy it, baby…you deserve it." Roman replied, right before she hurried out of the restaurant, to the elevators.

****

Shonda left the salon and spa sporting a fresh mani/pedi and feeling great from head to toe thanks to the hydra facial and full body deep tissue massage she'd received. When she got back to the room Roman was nowhere to be found, but there was a box and a note on the perfectly made bed.

Shonda picked up the note and read it out loud first.

Hey baby,

Had to step out and handle some things real quick. I know that massage has you feeling right. So, rest up for a while cause later we're gonna turn up in Atlantic City. Hopefully, my pre-birthday surprise will keep you motivated for what's in store tonight. Love You…Roman!

Shonda smiled, as she folded the note up and tore open the box. Inside was a brand-new cherry red cocktail dress, with matching cherry red Jusseippe shoes, and a purse to match. Shonda pulled out the dress, then walked over to the bathroom door and stood in front of the mirror.

"This is gonna look so good on me," Shonda said holding the dress to her body.

She laid the dress back down on the bed, then removed her clothes and went to take a long, hot shower. After her shower, she wrapped herself with a towel and laid down in the bed. Just as she was about to go to sleep she received a text on her phone.

She reached into the side of her purse she'd left on the bed, pulled out her phone and opened the message.

//: *Hey baby girl. I know you with yo' man, right now. But, I couldn't go any longer without wishing you a Happy Birthday. Just wanted you to know, I had to stop through Atlantic City on business. I'm at the Golden Nugget hotel, I remember you telling me that's where you staying this weekend. So, I was able to get a King Luxury Suite, Room 417. I miss you and I know you miss me, so bring that sexy ass to my room ASAP. I'll be waiting.*

//: *Thank You, Larenzo but my birthday isn't until tomorrow.*

//: *I know, figured you'd be busy tomorrow, wanted to go ahead and get mines in early.*

//: *Okay, thank you again. I will think about coming to see you but don't get your hopes up.*

//: *Yeah, right, you miss this big dick, so stop playing. I know your man ain't there. I saw him leave a few minutes ago. So, no excuses. Don't respond back just bring that ass on, while you still got time.*

Shonda laughed at Larenzo's comment, she read over the messages once more, then deleted them.

"What the hell, one last time can't hurt!" She said, exiting the room.

73

Chapter Eight

Larenzo laughed as he read their text messages again. He erased them, then dialed a phone number.

"What up?" The caller asked.

"'About to hit the gym," Larenzo answered. "What you doing?"

"Handling some things for later, but we're still on for tomorrow, don't worry. Stop calling before you fuck shit up."

Just then Larenzo heard a knock at the door.

"I'ma hit you back, later," Larenzo said quickly and hung up.

Larenzo tossed the phone in the chair by the window, and hurried through the living room, to answer the door.

"I knew you couldn't resist," Larenzo said, smiling arrogantly.

"Shut up, Jack ass," Shonda said, pushing him into the room, by his chest, as the door slammed shut behind them.

Shonda looked around the room at the grey furniture and the dazzling chandeliers hanging high in the ceiling.

"Nice suite," Shonda said.

Larenzo removed her hand from his chest and kissed the back of it. Shonda stared into his eyes, then he leaned in and kissed her, slipping his tongue into her mouth.

"Larenzo, I don't have time to be romantic and shit. I gotta get back before, Roman does."

"I'm not dumb, now turn around," Larenzo replied.

Shonda looked at him confused, without words, Larenzo turned her around facing the door. He held the back of her neck with one hand and lifted the skirt she was wearing with the other. A smile formed across his lips when he realized she wasn't wearing any panties. He put his middle finger inside her, feeling her wetness, and started pushing his finger in and out. Shonda threw her head back on Larenzo's shoulder and rest it.

"Oohhh…" Shonda moaned.

Larenzo leaned forward and grabbed her earlobe with his teeth. As he bit on her ear, he freed his inches, through the zipper of his pants. Then in a swift motion, as he bit her ear harder, and held her neck tighter, he entered her.

"Whose pussy is this?" Larenzo breathed into her ear, after releasing his hold on it.

"Unhhh…it's…it's yours!" Shonda moaned pressing her hands against the door, for leverage. "Take that pussy baby!" She squealed, as Larenzo's dick, pushed deeper inside her. "Don't knock my walls outta the frame. I will…will need them later." She shrieked, between breaths of pleasure.

"I…I…know, shush and let me do what I do." Larenzo groaned, entering deeper, slowing his strokes.

"Aaahhh…shit Larenzo…fuck me!" Shonda moaned, throwing back her hips. That massage she had earlier was everything and had her body feeling right.

"Work that pussy, faster," Larenzo demanded.

He pushed her forward, until her face was resting against the door, and went deeper. He ignored her request about taking it easy on her walls. "This is in case that nigga reneges." He said to himself, as a nut rushed through him.

"Aaahhh…sss…shit, Larenzo! Good…so fucking good!" Shonda moaned louder, as her body trembled, and an orgasm escaped her.

"God-damn, you feel good. Are you sure you have to leave so soon?" Larenzo asked as he pulled out to keep from bussing inside her.

Shonda pulled her skirt down and turned facing him. "Damn you don't get enough?" she asked kissing him.

Larenzo shook his head, "Nope, apparently you don't either. Do you?"

"You stupid." Shonda giggled.

She kissed him once more, then exited the room just as quickly as she'd entered. When she returned to her suite, she was relieved Roman hadn't returned yet.

"Thank God!" she said out loud, coming out of her clothes.

She grabbed her phone off the charger, seeing that she's missed a call from Roman. She checked the time, he'd called her right after she left the room to go see Larenzo. She jumped in the shower, to wash all evidence of her rendezvous with Larenzo off. After she finished showering, she went into her bag and retrieved the items she used to moisturize and scent her skin. She sat on the bed, press the code unlocking her phone, and called Roman.

As the phone ring, she squeezed lotion into her free hand and started massaging her legs one after the other.

"Hey baby, how was your massage?" Roman asked.

"It was great. I had to come back and take a nap," Shonda lied.

"I figured that much, I had to make reservations for tonight, then get a shape-up and trim. Can't have you be the only one looking good tonight. I'll see you in a few."

"Okay, I'll see you soon."

Shonda went back to her original task. She was dressed and ready, the minute Roman arrived.

77

"You look amazing," Roman said, grabbing Shonda's hand, pulling her over to him. "You smell good, too." Roman complimented.

Shonda stepped back and looked at him. "You kinda handsome yourself." she laughed.

"Kinda?" Roman repeated, locking eyes with her. "I look good, shit. I had to step my game up to stay on your level." Roman joked, pulling her back into him.

"You so silly." She laughed, then they locked lips.

Feeling steam rise between them, Roman released Shonda from his grip, she stepped back and grabbed her purse off the bed.

"So, where we going? I ain't get all jazzed up for nothing," Shonda stated.

"Let me shower real quick and change, then we'll be on our way," Roman said, heading towards the bathroom.

Shonda and Roman went to a lounge with live entertainment and an open bar, not too far from the hotel. As Shonda stood at the bar, waiting for the bartender to make her dirty Martini she heard a familiar voice behind her and as if she hadn't just fucked him a few hours ago, chills shot through her like lightning.

"Funny running into you here," he said.

"I can say the same for you," Shonda said, barely above a whisper as she turned facing Larenzo.

"You look good." Larenzo complimented, biting his bottom lip, eyeing her dress and shoes.

"Thanks, but you shouldn't be here," Shonda said nervously.

Larenzo scanned the room quickly, then looked back at Shonda pulling the hair on his chin. "It's a free country, oh shit oh boy must be here, right?"

"You already know he is, so quit playing." Shonda shot him a smirk.

"I ain't playing, but let me get outta here, wouldn't wanna cause issues with you and your man." Larenzo leaned in, pulled Shonda to him, then proceeded to kiss, but she quickly declined.

"Stop Larenzo," Shonda said backing away. She looked around making sure no one was watching.

"Oh…oh, my bad," Larenzo said, smiling. He raised his hands and backed up. "I'ma get outta here, call me when you get back home."

"Uh huh," Shonda said dismissing him.

Larenzo turned with a smug grin on his face. As he exited the lounge, he bumped into Roman. Shonda watched their interaction out of the corner of her eyes. She stood up and slowly trailed off in their direction, being sure they weren't aware of her presence.

****

"Have you lost your fuckin' mind, coming here?" Roman barked.

"Relax, I just stepped out to get a drink or two," Larenzo stated.

"And you had to do that shit here?" Roman wasn't convinced by Larenzo's excuse.

"Look, I'm headed out, so what's that problem?" Larenzo snapped.

"Cause you being seen by Shonda is damn risky, don't you think?" Roman asked.

"From her demeanor, she has no idea," Larenzo explained.

"I hope you're right cause the only way we're gonna do this without a hitch, is if she has no clue."

"Nigga, I told you, I got it. I can't wait until we get this shit over with tomorrow. So, I ain't gotta hear you bitching no more."

"Me too, matter of fact, how about we switch things up and get it done tonight." Roman offered.

"Tonight…why the sudden change?" Larenzo asked Roman.

"Well with you hanging around, it'll only be a matter of time before she starts getting suspicious," Roman said, pausing to look around making sure no one saw or heard them. "Shonda's smart, you know that shit. How the hell else could she get away with fucking both of us and neither one of us knew about it. We have to stay one step ahead of her…"

Larenzo raised his hand and nodded, "No need to beg nigga, just text me when you ready."

Larenzo and Roman talked for a more few minutes putting their plan together, then Larenzo left and Roman headed back towards the lounge.

****

After a couple of drinks, some dancing, and a little gambling, Roman was finally ready to leave. He eased his hand around Shonda's waist and pulled her close.

"You ready to go?" he asked.

"Yeah, why what you trying to get into?" Shonda asked, standing back eyeing him.

"The night is still young, so who knows," Roman replied, sliding his hand down over her ass, squeezing it, while he bit his bottom lips.

No words needed to be spoken, Shonda knew exactly what he was implying.

"Let's go, then." She said, removing his hand from her ass, walking back over to their table. She gathered her purse, finished the remainder of her dirty Martini, and sashayed towards the exit.

Roman followed behind her, eyeing her backside, licking his lips fighting the growing erection in his slacks. As promised before he ventured out of the exit doors he texted Larenzo. As they waited for the valet to bring the car around, Shonda looked up at the city skyline.

"You okay, babe?" Roman asked, moving over to her, wrapping his arms around her waist.

Shonda nodded and gave him a smile as bright as the lights, shining down on Atlantic City.

"It's so beautiful out here at night," Shonda said, referring to how the skyline was always lit up at night.

"It is beautiful, so are you." Roman kissed her softly.

"You know what I think I'm going to the suite to take a bubble and relax," Shonda replied smiling.

"Okay, good cause I want to get some gym time in before they close up for the night," Roman answered smiling also.

Shonda quickly rushed into the bathroom the minute they arrived back suite 319. She turned the faucet on, and let the water run, she brushed her teeth, while waiting for Roman to leave back out. When she heard the door close, she peeped out of the bathroom.

"Good showtime," She said, pulling her sexy lingerie out of her suitcase, along with the matching heels.

She turned the shower on and washed up. Afterward she scented her skin and text Roman to see how much longer he'd be. His response gave her the time she needed to finish getting fresh and sexy. Once she was dressed, she laid on top of the bed and waited patiently, anticipating the reaction she was bound to receive.

Chapter Nine

"Working on that stamina, huh?" Roman entered the gym interrupting Larenzo's push-up session.

"Nigga, please, I got stamina for days," Larenzo said, getting up off the floor. "So, where's the little lady?" He asked, smirking.

"In the room relaxing and taking a bubble bath. She should be done, by the time we get there." Roman answered.

Larenzo grabbed the towel off the bench and wiped his face and shirtless torso. He looked at Roman seriously, "Ro, one question, bruh."

"What?" Roman replied, giving him the same look.

"Have you thought about what happens after tonight?"

"What you mean?" Roman shrugged.

"Well, you'll be sharing the woman you say, you love, with another man..."

"I'm aware of that Larenzo, that's tomorrow's problem." Roman snapped, cutting him off. Roman didn't want to think about what would happen after tonight. He wasn't clueless to the reality, that after tonight, decisions...important ones would have to be made.

"Come on man, let's get this over with," Roman stated, nonchalant.

"You sound so excited," Larenzo replied, with a slight chuckle.

"Shut up," Roman snapped, pushing him towards the door.

Without any more conversation, they exited the gym and headed to room 319. Shonda heard the knob to the room door jiggle, then she assumed the position. When Larenzo and Roman entered the room, they stopped dead in their tracks and their mouths dropped wide open.

This right here's the panty-droppa
Whoa-oh, whoa-oh-oh-oh, yeah, whoa-uh
This right here's a baby maker...

The sounds of *Trey Songz Chapter 5* album filled the room. Shonda sat on the bed, legs crossed and glistening. Her breast nipples protruded through her outfit and an aroma delicious enough to entice any man in her vicinity flooded their noses. Shonda got up slowly exposing the entire lingerie set. She stood there with her hands on her hips and a smile on her face.

"What's wrong, fellas?" She asked looking from Roman, then over at Larenzo. "Don't stand there looking all shy and shit. This is what y'all wanted right?"

"Wh...what you talking about, Baby?" Roman stuttered.

"I know about your little plan Roman and Larenzo. So, now..." Shonda paused and rubbed her hand over her breasts. "Who's first?" She asked, walking over to the men, she took turns grabbing each of their dicks, both were hard as steel.

"Aahhh...shit fuck it," Larenzo spoke up, then picked Shonda up and carried her over to the bed.

Larenzo started kissing her, as his hands began sliding her top down. He moved down to her neck and sucked, as his hands roamed down to her center. He found her warmth and inserted two fingers inside. Roman stood there, mouth open, watching as Shonda and Larenzo wasted no time tearing into each other.

"Are you gonna stand there looking stupid, or you gonna come over here and join the fun?" Shonda asked, looking at Roman over Larenzo's shoulder.

Roman unbuttoned and removed his collared shirt, pulled his tee-shirt over his head, then unbuckled and dropped his pants. Once he was fully naked, he walked over to the side of the bed and climbed up on the mattress positioning her head toward his steel.

Shonda took his tip inside her mouth and as she went to work, bobbing her head up and down. Larenzo paused to remove all his clothes, then got down on his knees, pulled her lingerie bottom and thong off, and parted her thighs. He buried his head between her legs and started sucking on Shonda's clit, then slipped his fingers back inside her wetness.

As Shonda sucked and slobbed taking Roman's inches further into her mouth. Larenzo caused her legs to quiver as his tongue and fingers attacked her sweet spot relentlessly. Shonda and Roman released orgasms simultaneously, then Roman and Larenzo switched places. As Shonda took Larenzo's throbbing member into her mouth. Roman grabbed her legs and held them tight into the creases of his arms. He entered her with one quick, hard thrust pushing all his inches into her walls and went to work.

Shonda continued sucking and Roman continued stroking. While Larenzo took one of her breasts into his mouth and teased her nipple, with his tongue. The pleasure was so intense, Shonda had to stop sucking Larenzo's dick and scream out.

"Aahhh...fuck...," she shrieked loudly.

Just as she was about to go back to her previous task. She felt Larenzo's warm, sticky liquid all over her breasts.

Immediately after that, Roman pulled out and released his fluids on her stomach. As Roman stood stroking his dick, getting it hard again, Larenzo moved to the foot of the bed.

"Turn over and put that ass in the air. You know how I like it," Larenzo commanded.

Shonda gladly obliged his request. She stood up, before turning around, closed the space between her and Larenzo and kissed his lips, slipping her tongue into his mouth. Larenzo palmed her ass and squeezed it firmly. Roman couldn't help but notice the sexual chemistry between them. The way Shonda stared at Larenzo as if he was the best she'd ever had, was an eye-opening revelation.

"Hold up…" Roman interrupted loudly. "I'll be damned if I'm about to sit back and let y'all have all the fucking fun."

"Well bring your simple ass over here." Larenzo insulted.

"I have an idea that will make us all happy," Shonda interjected.

"Oh, yeah, what's that?" Roman asked, curious.

Shonda smiled seductively, she licked her lips as she walked over to Roman and took him by the hand. She led him over to the bed, then pushed him down on it.

"What are you doing, Shonda?" Larenzo asked also curious.

Shonda turned to him and placed two fingers over his lips. "Shush, I'm running shit now, got it?" Shonda looked from one man to the other. They eyed her and just nodded their heads. "Good, now watch me work."

Shonda removed the remainder of her clothes. Then she climbed on top of Roman and eased her wetness down onto his rock-hard shaft. When he was all the way in her, Shonda turned to Larenzo.

"Now take me from the back. You know what to do."

Larenzo wasted no time, retrieving the mango scented lubricant, he'd seen on the dresser when they entered the room. He squeezed two small drops on his tip, then squeezed a line down the crack of her ass. Once she was lubed enough and his dick was at its full potential, he slowly entered her forbidden treasure.

As Roman pounded her pussy, and Larenzo fucked her ass. Shonda felt an array of pain and pleasure that was so intense tears filled her eyes. It was her ultimate fantasy to have both her holes filled at the same time. Now that they were, she vowed to enjoy every second of every stroke and thrust. She pressed down into Roman's chest, gritted her teeth, and moved her body trying to keep up with the rhythm of their motions.

"Oohhh…uunnhhh…" she moaned, then reached back spreading her ass cheeks, so they'd both get the hint to go deeper.

Roman wrapped his arms around her and with one quick thrust he gave her every inch he had. Larenzo grabbed ahold of her love handles, held tight, and pushed so deep inside her forbidden treasure, she let out the loudest squeal he'd ever heard her make.

"Ooowww…" Shonda squealed, she shut her eyes and tears fell from them, but she didn't let that discourage her, she exhaled deeply and took it the best she could.

"Take that dick baby," Larenzo demanded.

"You like my dick?" Roman asked at the exact same time.

Shonda simply nodded her response. She moved faster as an orgasm began to rise inside of her. When her body started quivering, both Roman and Larenzo speeded their thrusts and fucked her harder. After releasing powerful orgasms almost simultaneously, Shonda was able to take a few moments to get her mind right before the next round, that was sure to come.

"You stalling or…" Roman was instantly cut off by the wave of her hand.

"Don't even try it, I ain't tapping out this far in the game," Shonda stated. "Matter of fact get your ass over here. I wanna feel your dick deep in my ass too."

"Yes ma'am," Roman joked, stroking his thickness back to attention.

"What you want me to do?" Larenzo inquired, also stroking his thickness.

Shonda didn't answer his question, instead, she got up off the bed and pushed Roman against the wall behind them, adjacent to the bathroom.

"Pick me up," she requested, looking back at Roman over her shoulder.

He did as he was told without hesitation and lifted her into his arms.

"Now spread my legs wide," Shonda instructed.

After her legs were spread, she reached down and grabbed his pulsating dick, then placed the tip at the crack of her ass. As Roman slowly pushed in and out of her, Shonda motioned with her finger for Larenzo. He quickly rushed over to her still holding his stiffness in his hand. No words were exchanged as Shonda grabbed his dick and placed it at the center of her dripping wet opening.

Larenzo put his inches deep inside her, he lifted one of her legs onto his shoulder, as Roman held tight to the other leg. Shonda wrapped her arms around Larenzo's neck and started kissing him. At the exact same time, Roman started sucking the back of her neck. Shonda began to sweat as she worked her body, she felt so good, she wanted to scream, but couldn't since Larenzo was tonguing her down like his life depended on it.

Tears fell from her eyes once again, and her body felt as though it was on fire as an orgasm surged through her. Her body shook and seemed to make both men more excited, as she felt both of dick get even harder. Each one intensified their strokes and pushed even more inches inside of her. Shonda had to hold tight to Larenzo's neck as another orgasm built up.

"Fuck baby, this some good pussy!" Larenzo moaned, after finally breaking their kiss, giving her more inches.

Shonda tried to pull her legs back, so she could regain control, but it was useless. Roman and Larenzo had vice grip holds on her legs.

"Don't try to run now..." Roman instructed fucking her harder. "This what you wanted, right?" he teased, licking the inside of her ear.

"Aahhh...God...ssshit...shit!" Shonda squealed, moving her hips faster while clenching her walls and ass in an attempt to make them cum quicker.

"I think she 'bout had enough, bro." Roman assumed.

Larenzo let out a slight chuckle and moaned, "You can't give up yet, Baby Girl...not until you make, Big Daddy cum." Larenzo said, kissing her once more. "Now talk dirty to me..."

"Fuck me harder, Daddy…Larenzo fuck this pussy, baby!" She screamed, then turned to Roman. "Aaahhh…yes…yy…yes. Take…take…that ass, Roman!"

Shonda's breathing increased as another orgasm threatened to drive her crazy. "Shit…f…fuck…fuck me!" she belted out, loud enough to wake the entire hotel.

"Say my name, baby," Larenzo requested.

"Unnhhh…La…Larenzo!" Shonda screamed.

"Now say mine," Roman demanded.

"Ro…Roman…oohhh…God…I…I…can't. I can't take no more!" Shonda finally admitted. "Oohhh…God…pl…please stop," she begged.

Seconds later they all released powerful orgasm together. No one moved until they were able to catch their breaths and Shonda's body had finally stopped trembling. Larenzo and Roman pulled their dicks out of her and released her legs. Shonda was so exhausted she almost collapsed to the floor, but Roman caught her and carried her back over to the bd.

After laying her down, he walked over to the mini-fridge and grabbed the spray can whip cream, he'd purchased when they first got there. He sprayed it all over her breasts covering her nipples. Then he sprayed some on her stomach and the remainder on her pussy. As Roman dropped to his knees and devoured her sweet nectar, Larenzo sucked her titties like an ice-cream cone on a hot summer day.

Shonda grabbed ahold of the back of Roman's head and held it in place as he licked all the whipped cream off her clitoris and pussy.

"Ummm…that…feels…sss…so good!" Shonda moaned, allowing them to take her all the way to ecstasy over and over, and over again.

Chapter Ten

Later that morning when Shonda awoke her body was still exhausted and sore from the pain and pleasure she'd endured. She struggled to sit up, then looked around the room. She didn't see Roman or Larenzo anywhere, but just as she was about to get out of bed, Roman came into the room, carrying a white foam carry-out tray.

"Good morning got you some breakfast," Roman said. "Figured you'd be hungry after last night."

Shonda was sure she'd heard a hint of disdain in his voice. "Something wrong, Roman?" she asked.

Roman quietly handed her the tray, Shonda opened it and dug into the pancakes and eggs, waiting for his response. After finishing her first bite, she turned back to Roman, who was now sitting in the chair, with his eyes fixated on the black T.V. screen. This confirmed that something was up with him.

"Roman, what's your problem?"

"How long you been fucking, Larenzo?" He bluntly asked, shooting his eyes in her direction.

Shonda was so caught off guard, she almost choked on her food. "Why...why you asking me that now, Roman? You didn't seem to care last night."

"I did care, but I'd made a deal with the devil... meaning my brother, I couldn't back out of. He would have never let me live it down," Roman admitted.

"What's with this whole rivalry shit, between y'all anyway. I've never known twins to hate each other so much."

"It's been like that for years. I guess our parents are to blame, they made him their golden child. He was always the best looking, most athletic, got the best grades. Hell, he even stayed home after high school to help my dad's business stay afloat after he got sick. Then when pops died Renzo took over and made sure mom and the business was good. They have never forgiven me for abandoning them as they call it. I have always been known as the black sheep. Larenzo always made it his mission to prove he was the stronger and better man between us. Even last night, despite my best efforts he still reigned…"

"How you figure that?" Shonda instantly cut him off.

"I saw the chemistry between you two. The way you said his name. The way you took his dick…in ways you've never done with me. Before last night I never fucked you in the ass before, but you were very comfortable when Larenzo did it. Which tells me it wasn't his first time."

"Roman, that's not my fault, Larenzo brought out of me things you refused to do."

"Oh, so it's my fault you fucked around on me for the past four months with my fucking brother?"

"Roman, I'm sorry, I never meant to hurt you. It just happened. I was alone at Bike Fest, he was there, and he looked out for me then one thing led to another…" Shonda tried to explain.

"Let me guess his dick just fell in your pussy, right? And you let it happen over and over again. Now it all makes sense…the bruises on your ass. The scratches on your wrists…" Roman made finger quotes in the air. "The constant out of town clients. Do you even have clients out of town?"

"Yes, Roman, I do," Shonda replied.

"Yeah right," Roman snapped.

Shonda could see the anger building up and the tears he was trying to hold back.

"Roman, what are you getting at?" Shonda was anxious to end this conversation once and for all.

"Look let me be clear, last night was a pleasurable, yet eye-opening experience. Bottom line Shonda...the days of you going back and forth with and me that nigga are over. It's either me or him." Roman stood on the edge of the bed, arms folded, waiting for an answer.

Shonda looked at him, she opened her mouth, but no sound came out. She wanted to tell him, she loved him and wanted him only. But she couldn't, the fact was they both had traits she enjoyed.

"That's exactly what the fuck I thought." Roman barked angrily. He pulled the hotel key from his back pocket and tossed them at her feet on the bed.

"What are you doing, Roman?" Shonda asked confused.

"I'm leaving, I already put my things in a cab downstairs. I figured you either wouldn't choose or you'd choose Larenzo. So, the room is still paid for another two days. I'm sure you'll find a way to use it to your advantage since Larenzo is sniffing around here somewhere. I refuse to be second best to that motherfucking brother of mine...again. I hope y'all have a great fucking life together." Without another word, Roman stormed out of the bedroom, and exited the suite, slamming the door behind him.

Shonda wanted to get up and run behind him to explain she didn't want to lose him, despite how he felt, but the soreness she felt made it complicated to move. So, she just sat there with her mouth drop and her mind racing with confusion.

One Week Later...

"You never told me what happened in Atlantic City," Nina said sitting across from Shonda's desk.

"Girl, it was crazy and wild. I'll just leave it at that." Shonda replied with a sneaky grin.

"Ah, hell what did you do, with your nasty ass?" Nina knew Shonda was hiding something.

"I told you how I wanted to feel both of them inside of me, right?" Shonda reminded.

"Yeah," Nina shrugged.

Shonda's smiled grew wider, "Well I got my wish...it was some hot steamy birthday fucking going on in that suite." Shonda's pussy got wet and throbbed just thinking back on that night.

"Oh, wow, you, slutty whore!" Nina laughed.

"Shut up," Shonda also laughed.

"I can't believe you pulled it off, though." Nina was still shocked.

"Them fools thought they were gonna catch me slipping. I flipped that shit back on them."

"Good for you. So, what happened after that?"

"To make a long story short, Roman dumped me and I cut ties with Larenzo. Shit after a night like that, there's no going back," Shonda admitted.

She'd experienced her deepest desire. Now it was on to the next mission and the next late-night lick fantasy with someone new and preferably shy and naïve, so she could tame them in the bedroom, just as Larenzo had tamed her from the first night they fucked, until the very last.

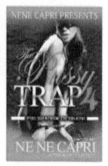

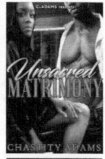

NENE CAPRI PRESENTS

Available in Paperback..!!

The Pussy Trap series 1 -5
Trust No Bitch series 1-3
Tainted 1 & 2
Diamonds Pumps & Glocks
Late Night Lick Vol. 1, 5, 6, 8, 10, 11
By NeNe Capri

Chastity Adams Presents

Gangsta Lovin' 1 & 2
Love Sex & Mayhem 1 & 2
Treacherous Desire
Late Night Lick Vol. 2, 4, 7 & 9
Unsacred Matrimony
By Chastity Adams

We Ship to Prisons:
Po Box 741581
Riverdale, GA 30274